Baby Lessons

TERI WILSON

HARLEQUIN
SPECIAL
EDITION

Recycling programs for this product may not exist in your area.

ISBN-13: 978-1-335-89468-7

Baby Lessons

Copyright © 2020 by Teri Wilson

This edition published by arrangement with Harlequin Books S.A.

For questions and comments about the quality of this book, please contact us at CustomerService@Harlequin.com.

Harlequin Enterprises ULC
22 Adelaide St. West, 40th Floor
Toronto, Ontario M5H 4E3, Canada
www.Harlequin.com

Printed in U.S.A.

Madison's gaze slid toward the babies in the tub and then back toward him. "I suppose I owe you a thank-you. I was beginning to think I'd make a terrible mother someday, but now…"

"There's more to being a mother than knowing how to change a diaper, Madison. Simply showing up is a hell of a good start."

Jack wasn't sure which one of them leaned in first or if they'd simply been drawn to each other by some invisible force, but she was suddenly right there, just a whisper away, so close that he could see the heat in her eyes, as precious and unexpected as liquid gold.

He cupped her cheek in one of his hands—the lightest of touches, but it sent shock waves of awareness coursing through him, warm like honey. "You'll make a wonderful mother. Trust me."

"I trust you," she whispered, and the last shred of Jack's resistance fell away.

His gaze dropped to her perfect pink mouth and he dipped his head toward hers. Somehow Jack summoned the wherewithal to send her a questioning look, because as much as he wanted this, he needed to know she wanted it, too.

She nodded, lips parting, and every cell in his body seemed to cry with relief.

* * *

**LOVESTRUCK, VERMONT:
Welcome to the loveliest town in Vermont!**

Dear Reader,

Welcome to Lovestruck, Vermont, my brand-new series for Harlequin Special Edition! *Baby Lessons* is the first in a four-book series about newcomers to a charming small town where love comes in packages. My hope is that you'll have a big smile on your face as you read Madison and Jack's story. You might even shed a tear or two.

Our hero in this book, Jack Cole, is a fireman. I've wanted to write a book featuring a firefighter for a really long time because my stepdad, Lanny Cunningham, is a retired firefighter who worked for the Los Angeles Fire Department for many years.

Displaced big-city fashionista Madison Jules meets Lieutenant Jack Cole when she nearly burns a barn down with her hair straightener. The next time she runs into him isn't any less awkward, so when she applies for a part-time job as the night nanny for his infant twin daughters, he's not exactly thrilled to hire her. But Madison and Jack are both hiding an important secret, so there are much bigger problems at hand than the fact that Madison doesn't know how to change a diaper. They make such a great couple, though. I had so much fun writing about their shenanigans.

I hope you enjoy this little trip to the Vermont countryside. As always, thank you so much for reading. And please look for the next book in the Lovestruck series—more firefighters!—coming this Christmas.

Happy reading!

Teri Wilson

Teri Wilson is a *Publishers Weekly* bestselling author of romance and romantic comedy. Several of Teri's books have been adapted into Hallmark Channel Original Movies, most notably *Unleashing Mr. Darcy*. She is also a recipient of the prestigious RITA® Award for excellence in romantic fiction for her novel *The Bachelor's Baby Surprise*. Teri has a major weakness for cute animals and pretty dresses, and she loves following the British royal family. Visit Teri at teriwilson.net.

Books by Teri Wilson

Harlequin Special Edition

Furever Yours

How to Rescue a Family

Wilde Hearts

The Ballerina's Secret
How to Romance a Runaway Bride
The Bachelor's Baby Surprise
A Daddy by Christmas

Drake Diamonds

His Ballerina Bride
The Princess Problem
It Started with a Diamond

HQN

Unmasking Juliet
Unleashing Mr. Darcy

Visit the Author Profile page
at Harlequin.com for more titles.

For Lanny, our family's real-life firefighter hero.

With special thanks to Captain Jeremy Huntsman
and San Antonio Fire Station 34 for all the
amazing research help and inspiration!

Chapter One

Vermont hates me.

It was an undeniable fact. Nothing had gone right in the ten days since Madison Jules had relocated from Manhattan to Lovestruck, Vermont. Not one single thing.

Seriously, why?

She squinted at her reflection in the mirror, trying to assess the situation as best she could in the semi-darkness. Even without electricity, she could tell that it was bad. Half her hair was smoothed into a perfect glossy bob, while the other half was a mass of uncontrollable curls. And since the power clearly had no intention of returning, things probably weren't going to improve anytime soon.

Perfect. Just perfect. She was going to have to go to the office like this. But first, she was going to have to deal with whoever had decided to pound on her door at six thirty in the morning.

Six thirty! If Vermont was an individual human instead of a geographic location, it would be a morning person. Yet another thing it didn't have in common with Madison.

"Coming!" She shuffled to the door in her favorite Kate Spade slippers—the cute velvet ones that said Eat Cake for Breakfast—and wrapped her polka dot robe more tightly around her frame. "Aunt Alice, if it's you, do you have electricity up at the main house? Because I sure don't."

It wasn't her aunt, as Madison found out when she swung the door open to reveal a fireman dressed in full firefighter regalia—bulky jacket with reflective trim, heavy pants, scuffed black boots. A fire helmet was jauntily positioned on his head, perfectly angled to accentuate the scowl on his face.

Maybe she wasn't the only nonmorning person in Vermont, after all. Finally, someone who understood her.

"Hi," Madison said, peering past him in search of flames. Her aunt's house looked perfectly unscathed, thank goodness. "Where's the fire?"

"In your apartment," he said flatly.

"What?" She shook her head. A copper ringlet from the left side of her hair fell across her eyes, and she blew it out of the way. "There's no fire."

"I'm afraid there is," he countered.

Seriously? She would know if her own apartment was on fire. Perched in her aunt's barn, it wasn't exactly spacious—barely larger than her fourth-floor walk-up in New York. But very much *unlike* her former big city digs, her Vermont apartment was rent-free. So she had no problem whatsoever with its close quarters. Bonus: if any part of it were aflame, she would definitely know.

"No, really. There's not. I was in the middle of flat-ironing my hair and the electricity went out, that's all." She tilted her head to properly accentuate her hair's good side.

The fireman remained unimpressed. "A heat sensor in this building activated an alarm at the fire station. I need to come in and take a look around."

"Okay." Madison blinked as she held the door open wide and he strode past her. "But…"

He carried a fire extinguisher in one hand and an ax rested on one of his broad shoulders. How had Madison missed the ax? Her hair mishap was beginning to seem less and less important. It was official—Vermont had finally broken her.

She shifted from one slippered foot to the other,

acutely aware of just how ridiculous she must look. Probably because there was suddenly a cranky yet attractive fireman filling up the tiny space of her apartment. "Um. What's with the ax? You're not going to hack away at my walls, are you?"

Because technically, they weren't really her walls at all. They were Aunt Alice's, and for some reason, it seemed like a bad thing to have them destroyed on her watch—even if the one doing the destroying was a heroic firefighter-type figure.

Not that Firefighter Cranky Pants struck Madison as remotely heroic at the moment. Weren't firemen supposed to be nice? Or at least somewhat pleasant? Particularly to people whose apartments were on— invisible—fire?

"I cut off all power to the building," someone said.

Madison turned to see another burly man in weighty fireproof clothing standing in the doorway. Oh goody, there were two of them. At least this one was smiling at her.

"Good morning, ma'am." The new arrival nodded. "I assume Lieutenant Cole informed you that an alarm sounded at the station and up at the main house a few minutes ago?"

"Sort of." Madison shot an accusatory glare at the grumpy one—Lieutenant Cole, apparently—but he was too busy glowering at her flat iron to notice.

"He mentioned an alarm, but I didn't realize it went off at the main house."

Aunt Alice must have headed out for an early-morning coffee before opening up the yarn store she owned on Main Street. Had she been home, she definitely would've let Madison know a fire alarm had sounded.

"The heat sensor for this building is wired to signal an alarm at the farmhouse rather than here." The fireman made a circular motion with his pointer finger, indicating Madison's living space. "The barn."

Right, as if she needed a reminder that she'd gone from living three blocks off Madison Avenue to sleeping in a barn. Technically, it was a tiny area *above* the barn—more like a garage apartment than a hayloft—but still.

"You sure you didn't see any flames? Not even a flash?" Lieutenant Cole arched a brow as he aimed his flashlight at the plug closest to her bathroom vanity. The plastic plate covering the outlet was covered in dark soot.

Madison blinked, horrified. "Oh my gosh. I... um...no."

Her back had been facing the outlet when the lights flickered before going out entirely. Shouldn't she have heard something, though? Had this grumpy public servant been right, and she'd failed to notice an actual fire in her home?

The indignities were multiplying by the second, but Madison no longer cared. The thought of the barn burning down around her was terrifying, to say the least.

"Is this the part where you use that?" She winced in the general direction of the ax.

Lieutenant Cole's frown deepened as if the struggle to fight off an eye roll was causing him physical pain. What *was* his problem? "No need. The flame burned itself out."

"How can you know that for sure?" She swallowed hard.

He sighed and crooked a finger at her, beckoning her forward.

She took a tentative step, butterflies swarming low in her belly. If she didn't know better, she would have mistaken the feeling for attraction. But that was impossible, obviously. It was probably just a normal reaction to her recent near-death experience, even though she hadn't actually been aware she was experiencing it.

Lieutenant Cole sighed again, regarding her with piercing blue eyes.

Madison's mouth went dry as the butterflies beat their wings even harder. What was happening?

"May I?" He flicked a finger toward her wrist.

He wanted to hold hands? High-five? What was

going on, and why was she suddenly mesmerized by the square set of his jaw?

Her hand drifted toward his, seemingly of its own accord. He took it, placed her palm flush against the wall and held it in place with his own manly grasp. "Feel anything?"

Goose bumps cascaded up and down her arm. She felt *everything* all of a sudden. Every*thing*. Every*where*.

"Um," was all she could manage to articulate and to her complete and utter horror, her gaze drifted toward his mouth. He had a small scar near the corner of his upper lip. Madison wondered if it might be the result of some heroic act during a fire.

Then she wondered if she might be having a stroke, because *what* was she doing?

She forced her gaze away from his perfect bone structure and back toward her hand, still flat against the wall with Lieutenant Cole's strong fingers ringing her wrist like a bracelet.

"Heat," he clarified. "Does the wall feel hot at all to you?"

"No." She shook her head.

"That's how I know." He dropped her wrist and shrugged. "If the flash hadn't burned itself out, either a fire would be visible or the Sheetrock would be warm, indicating a flame inside the wall."

Madison nodded. "Obviously."

"But if you really want us to *hack away* at your walls, that could be arranged." He narrowed his gaze, studying her for a moment until a hint of amusement crept its way into his eyes. Then Madison caught a glimpse of herself in the mirror behind him and realized he was looking at her mismatched hair.

"That won't be necessary." Good grief, he was annoying. She was willing to bet whatever was going on beneath his fire helmet wasn't much better than her current half-done mess.

She flashed him a triumphant grin, fantasizing about the state of his helmet hair.

But then, as smoothly as if he'd just read her mind, Lieutenant Cole removed his helmet and raked his hand through a head of dark, lush waves. He looked like he'd walked straight out of a shampoo commercial. Or one of those sexy firefighter calendars.

It was maddening.

"Are we done here?" she said tartly.

"Yes, ma'am. You'll need to get an electrician out here to replace your outlet." He jammed the helmet back on his head and then pointed at her flat iron. "Don't use that thing anymore. It's not safe."

"It's from Sephora," she said, but he'd already begun walking away, covering the distance from her vanity to the front door in three easy strides.

The other fireman—the nice one—smiled at

Madison as Lieutenant Cole brushed past him. "Sorry for the intrusion."

She glared at the lieutenant's back, silently cursing both her lingering butterflies and his fine head of hair.

"Is your colleague always so charming?" she said, injecting her voice with a massive dose of sarcasm.

The fireman offered her a conciliatory smile. "Again, my apologies. If you experience any more trouble, please give us a call."

He turned to follow Lieutenant Cole back to the fire engine parked at the foot of the gravel drive, where two additional firemen stood waiting and a crowd of curious onlookers had gathered. Odd. In New York, no one paid attention to flashing lights.

But Madison wasn't in her beloved New York anymore. Clearly.

She shut the door and fought her sudden urge to cry by channeling all of her energy into disliking the smug lieutenant and his smug, handsome face. On some level, she knew she was overreacting. But after ten days of trying her best to look on the bright side…to pick up the pieces of her shattered life and move on…she just couldn't do it anymore. Vermont had won. She needed to find a way to get her life back. She didn't belong here—that was the real emergency. Somebody call 911.

The nice fireman's parting words rang loudly in her consciousness as she picked up her flat iron.

If you experience any more trouble, please give us a call.

She hurled the hair appliance in the trash with more force than was probably necessary. But seriously, like she'd even want to risk having to call for help and roll out the welcome mat for the perfectly coifed Lieutenant Cole?

Not in this lifetime.

Lieutenant Jack Cole was dreaming.

It was a bothersome dream, plagued by a nagging voice, the sort that would ordinarily drag him back to wakefulness. But he hadn't slept in such a long time—weeks, months, *years*—so he fought it. He fought it hard.

Just closing his eyes felt so damn good, even better than he remembered. He just wanted to ride it out. Go with it. Let the dream take him wherever it wanted if he could just keep sleeping for ten more minutes. Five. Anything.

"Dude." Someone snapped his fingers in Jack's face. "Wake up. I'm talking to you."

With no small amount of reluctance, he cracked one eye open and realized he wasn't dreaming at all. He'd fallen asleep on the rig. Again. The annoying voice that kept breaking through the heavy fog of sleep belonged to the firefighter sitting across from him as the engine bounced along the rural road back to the station.

And now that firefighter was shaking his head and eyeing him with sympathy. Jack wished he could close his eyes again. He'd seen enough pitying glances aimed his direction over the past six months to last him a lifetime.

"You've got to get some sleep, man," Wade said. "Either that or take another leave of absence."

Jack shook his head. "Not an option."

He was a firefighter. It's what he did, and he was damn good at it. Or he used to be, back when sleep was a thing that happened with any sort of regularity.

"Well, you can't keep nodding off on the rig. At least wait until we get back to the station where there's a recliner with your name on it," Wade shouted above the jostle of the engine.

Jack shouldn't have been able to sleep through such a noisy ride, especially in one of the jump seats. No one should. Firefighters sometimes carried earplugs for this very purpose.

He scrubbed his hand over his face and did his best not to succumb to his near-constant overwhelming feeling of exhaustion. The passing scenery helped, but only marginally. Wade was right. He couldn't go on like this.

"Speaking of things you probably shouldn't be

doing…" Wade jerked his head in the direction of the farmhouse and accompanying barn with its converted apartment space where they'd just completed their first call of the morning. "What was that back there?"

"What do you mean?" Jack narrowed his gaze.

Their captain and the driver were situated in the cab of the truck behind Wade. The call at the farmhouse had been simple enough that they hadn't needed more than two team members to take a look around. Good thing, since there hadn't been room for any more people in the tiny apartment.

Wade shot him a knowing look. "Come on, man. You weren't yourself just now. Don't you think you were a bit harsh?"

"Harsh?" Jack shook his head. "No. You weren't there when I first knocked on her door. She tried to argue with me about whether or not there was a problem when, in fact, her fancy hair straightener almost burned the place down."

"You mean the one from Sephora?" Wade deadpanned.

Jack laughed, despite his foul mood.

"Seriously, though. You could have been nicer." Wade held on to his seat belt as the engine rounded the curve leading back to the station. "Or at the very least, civil."

"I was perfectly civil," Jack said. Granted, he

hadn't exactly been chatty, but he'd done his job. What more did Wade want from him?

"Don't you think she seemed a little…" Wade's brows rose, prompting Jack to fill in the blank.

"Out of place?" Granted, she'd been beautiful—in a just-rolled-out-of-bed sort of way. But she'd had *big city* written all over her. It was practically stamped across her forehead. "Yeah. Definitely."

"That's not what I meant at all." Wade frowned. "I was going to say she seemed vulnerable."

The engine slowed to a stop in front of the familiar red brick building decorated with a large American flag blowing just below block letters that spelled out Engine Co. 24. They idled for a moment until the diesel engine powered down with a prolonged whoosh that almost made it seem like the big red truck had sighed. Jack could relate—he felt like sighing himself.

"Vulnerable?" He let out a sharp laugh as he unfastened the buckle of his harness and hopped down from the jump seat. "I don't think so. She's a grown woman. Adults aren't vulnerable. *Babies* are vulnerable."

The second the words left his mouth, he wanted to swallow them up again and reel them back to the place where he kept all his frustration buried deep. Talking about it didn't help matters. So far, the only thing that had made him feel better about his current difficulties were the ridiculous letters he'd been writing lately. They were strangely cathartic, and they weren't hurting anyone.

Were they?

For a brief moment Jack wondered what Wade would have to say if he knew about his recent correspondence. Nothing good, that was for sure.

"You're right. Babies are indeed vulnerable." Wade shrugged out of his turnout gear as they walked toward the station. "But I don't think you noticed how that woman back there looked at you. I sure did."

Jack just shook his head. Maybe she'd seemed a little lonely, standing there all wide-eyed in her polka dot bathrobe. Jack recognized loneliness when he saw it. Hell, he knew that feeling better than anyone.

He'd even caught a glimmer of a spark between them when their fingertips touched. But a spark didn't mean anything other than a simple transfer of electrons. It was just science, and as Jack knew all too well, sometimes a spark could set off a burning rain of destruction.

No, thank you. Not again.

"Not all women are like Natalie, you know," Wade said. The earnestness in his voice made Jack's head hurt.

"Never mind," Jack muttered.

He'd said too much. He knew better than to drag his daughters into this conversation.

Adults aren't vulnerable. Babies *are vulnerable.*

Why hadn't he just kept his head down and his mouth shut? Now he was sure to be on the receiving end of more pitying looks from Wade. The rest of the guys at the station, too.

He could feel Wade's gaze on him even now, weighted down with concern. He didn't dare look up.

Jack didn't need anyone's pity. He had a roof over his head, food on his table and two precious babies waiting for him at home. Other than being a little sleep deprived, he was perfectly fine. Not lonely. Not wounded. Not miserable.

Certainly not vulnerable…

Even if he almost felt that way, every now and then.

Chapter Two

Just like everything else in Lovestruck, the office for the local newspaper bore no resemblance whatsoever to its Manhattan counterpart.

Before Madison's charmed life had been so rudely interrupted by the horrors of corporate downsizing, she used to walk past the New York Times building on a semiregular basis. Honestly, it was impossible to miss, even from a distance. It loomed over the midtown skyline, its sleek gray exterior as strong and serious as a pinstriped suit.

Not so in small-town Vermont. If the building that housed the Lovestruck paper had been an outfit, it would have been a seersucker sundress…with a wide-brimmed hat. Tucked neatly between her aunt's yarn store and the post office on Main Street, where every storefront was painted its own bright hue, the newspaper operated out of a cheery blue space with lemon-yellow trim. Even its name was ridiculous— the *Lovestruck Bee*.

Seriously, what did that even mean?

Madison didn't know, and nor did she care. It wasn't as if she aspired to climb whatever quaint, homespun career ladder existed at the *Bee*. She didn't dream of running the place someday, or—heaven forbid—being named senior editor of her section. She hadn't spent four years at Columbia followed by four more as a lowly assistant at *Vogue* before finally seeing her byline on the magazine's glossy pages in order to throw it all away and live in a barn. Not even a barn that was rent-free, thanks to Aunt Alice.

Madison was grateful for the help. Life in New York hadn't come cheap, and while she had more designer dresses and Jimmy Choo stilettos than she could count courtesy of the infamous Vogue "closet"—which, in reality, was even larger than depicted in movies and TV shows like *The Devil Wears Prada* and *Sex and the City*—she had next to nothing in her bank account. Getting laid off had never been part of the plan. Neither had her recent job search, which felt more like *The Hunger Games* than an interview process. As it turned out, "a million girls would kill for this job" wasn't just a movie catchphrase.

She'd needed a soft place to land. It had been years since Madison spent summer vacations visiting her aunt in Vermont. She wasn't sure she'd even seen Alice since her father's funeral, but she'd always had an open invitation to stay at the farmhouse and desperate times called for desperate measures. Aunt Alice encouraged her to apply for a job at the *Bee* right away, but Madison had put it off as long as she could. By the time she'd finally relented, she'd been so beaten down by failed job interviews that she'd been thrilled to get her own column...

Until her editor told her what she'd be writing about.

But it was okay. Really, it was. Relocating to Lovestruck was never meant to be permanent. She was simply biding her time here until she could get her real career back on track. Any day now, she'd get the call and she'd be back in the world of high fashion where she belonged.

Meanwhile, she was the *Lovestruck Bee*'s resident parenting expert. Oh, the irony.

"Madison, I realize the column is new for you—" Floyd Grant, her boss, sighed mightily as he peered at her over the top of his wire-rimmed reading glasses "—but we can't continue like this."

Madison took a deep breath, more than prepared to make the case for yesterday's column. "The Top Ten Infants to Follow on Instagram" had been more than thorough. She'd worked hard on that story. It had been listicle gold, and the photos she'd embedded from the top baby influencer accounts were beyond precious. The Manhattan mommy circuit would have gobbled up every word she'd written.

"Mr. Grant, I..."

Her words drifted off as he picked up a sheet of paper covered in familiar handwriting and dangled it mere inches from her face.

She swallowed hard. "Is that..."

"Another one?" He slammed the letter down on his desk and slid it toward her. "Yes. The second one this week, in fact."

She glanced down at the missive just long enough to spot the words *frivolous*, *vapid* and *fraud*. The first two didn't bother her much. If there was one thing that came in handy as a *Vogue* reporter, it was a thick skin. She'd grown accustomed to critics who didn't understand the social and cultural importance of fashion. The third word, however, made her stomach churn—probably because it was dead accurate.

Fraud.

Madison didn't know the first thing about parenting. Nor did she know anything about babies or toddlers or any other variety of children. But in her defense, she'd never claimed to be a modern-day Fred Rogers. She would have been the first one to admit that she knew more about Mr. Rogers's cardigans than she did about any of the kiddos who lived in his neighborhood. She could have whipped up a few thousand words on his sneakers alone.

But that was not what Floyd Grant and the good people of Lovestruck wanted from her. During her interview, she'd lobbied hard to write about something else...*anything* else. She might have even begged, but Mr. Grant stood firm. It was the parenting column or nothing at all. And judging by the look on his grizzled face, he was beginning to wish she'd opted for the latter.

"Please, Mr. Grant." She flashed him her brightest smile, which probably would have been more effective if she'd been able to rebound from the flat-iron disaster. She didn't feel like herself with her unkempt do. And she definitely didn't look like herself.

Worst. Day. Ever.

A wayward curl fell in front of her eyes and she made a valiant, yet ultimately unsuccessful, effort to tuck it behind her ear. "I don't know who keeps writing these letters complaining about my column, but odds are this disgruntled person is nothing but a troll."

"Excuse me?" Her boss's eyebrows rose.

Madison blinked. So now she was going to have to explain internet slang to her editor-in-chief. "A troll. It means someone who intentionally tries to start arguments online, usually just for the sake of getting attention."

"But this—" he jabbed at the letter with his pointer finger "—isn't simply an online comment. It's a letter to the editor, and you know what that means."

"You're going to print it, aren't you?"

"I don't have a choice." He shook his head. "It's *Bee* policy to print every letter to the editor."

Madison was aware. She'd just sort of hoped the policy had changed after the previous three letters had gone to press.

She stared at the most recent one, marveling yet again at the fact that someone had taken the time to complain about her column in longhand and send it to the *Bee* via snail mail. This wasn't a garden variety troll. Madison couldn't help but admire his or her persistence.

His, she thought. That boxy lettering seemed distinctly masculine, especially the aggressive little cross marks on the z's. Her attention snagged on the twin letters, and she made the mistake of reading the entire sentence.

It's puzzling to me why the author of the parenting column seems to care more about aesthetics than actual children.

Her throat grew thick, and to her complete and

utter horror, tears blurred her vision. Ugh, why was she letting a stupid troll get to her?

"I care about children," she said quietly.

She wasn't a monster, for crying out loud. Parenting just wasn't something that came naturally to someone whose own mom had passed away before she took her first steps.

"Of course you do." Something in Mr. Grant's gaze softened. He leaned back in his chair and rubbed a hand over his face. "But you've got to change things up. Your *troll* is calling for your resignation if you can't come up with any practical childcare advice."

"My *resignation*?" Nope. Not happening.

The only thing that would look worse on her résumé than writing for a small-town paper would be writing for no one at all. At least she had her own column, even if she wasn't allowed to use her actual name on the byline. Instead, the *Bee*'s readers knew her simply as Queen Bee. Super professional. Still, she couldn't screw it up. She just couldn't.

"I'm not quitting." She shook her head. Another loose curl fell into her field of vision, but this time she didn't bother trying to smooth it back into place. "I'll write something more hands-on. I promise."

Maybe she'd come up with a recipe or something. Kiddie cookout? Brunch for babies?

Gosh, she was hopeless.

"Might I make a suggestion?" Mr. Grant said.

Please do. Madison nodded.

"Spend some time with real kids." He waved a hand toward the window in his office overlooking Main Street as if some kind of toddler parade was taking place outside. "Honestly, it's the best thing you could possibly do."

She opened her mouth and then closed it again.

This wasn't the sort of advice she'd anticipated. She'd expected a list of possible column topics or maybe some actual editorial guidance. But no, her boss wanted her to babysit.

"Trust me. Do it, and your column will practically write itself." He glanced down at the letter and then back at her, and his expression hardened into a tight smile. "I hate to say this, but your job just might depend on it."

One of the things Jack liked best about being a fireman was the sense of camaraderie among the firefighters. A station was often referred to as a firehouse for a reason—the men and women who worked there functioned as a unit. They worked together, they exercised together, they ate together. Heck, they even slept together in one big dormitory-style bedroom outfitted with bunk beds.

They had rules, like no cell phones or tablets during mealtime. They binge-watched the same shows from the double rows of recliners facing the giant flat screen in the station's community living room. They went on grocery runs together and kept a chores chart outlining who was responsible for meal prep and cleanup during shifts.

The twelve firefighters who operated out of Lovestruck's sole station were a true band of brothers. They worked in teams—A, B or C—with each team pulling a twenty-four-hour shift, followed by forty-eight hours off duty. Jack was on the C team, as was his friend Wade and the other two firefighters who'd responded to the hair-related emergency out at the barn on the outskirts of town yesterday morning. The four men had been working the C shift together for years, so yeah, they were basically family.

It also meant they felt perfectly comfortable commenting on Jack's personal life at any given time. Ah, the joys of family.

Jack cracked eggs into a mixing bowl while Wade, Brody and Jason, whom they only ever called Cap—short for Captain—discussed his chaotic home life as if he wasn't even present. As usual, they all had a few choice words to say about Natalie. Jack did his best to tune them out and concentrate on the swirl of yellow egg yolks in the bowl, even though he'd made breakfast casserole so many times that he could have probably done it in his sleep.

Natalie was gone, and she wasn't coming back.

The signed divorce papers that had arrived on his doorstep on the very day the twins had turned two months old were a pretty firm indication that his marriage was over. What was there left to say on the matter?

"Enough about Natalie. It's time for Jack to move on," Wade said. "I keep telling him that, but he won't listen."

"I hear you loud and clear," Jack muttered, tossing a few handfuls of ground sausage into his batter. "I just disagree. Vehemently."

He'd already had to delete the dating app from his phone that the guys had installed during one of Jack's many impromptu naps. *Twice*. When were they going to take the hint?

"Look, we know you're stretched for time. But maybe if you had some sort of semblance of a personal life, you'd be more pleasant to be around." Cap unfolded the firehouse's copy of the *Lovestruck Bee*, snagging the sports page before anyone else had a chance to claim it.

Okay, then. Wade wasn't the only one who thought Jack was a jerk. His boss agreed. Note taken.

Jack stirred the egg mixture with a little too much force. "I have a life, thank you very much."

If anything, he had too much life. Too much responsibility. Not that he didn't love his twins. Jack's love for his girls ran deep—so deep it almost scared him sometimes. He couldn't imagine life without them. All he needed was a few uninterrupted nights' sleep and he'd be right as rain.

At work, what little sleep he got was interrupted by emergency calls, and at home…well, he couldn't remember the last time he'd slept for more than two consecutive hours in his own bed. Surely, the twins would start sleeping through the night soon. He hoped so, anyway. A man could dream.

Dream.

He blinked, suddenly remembering the strange dreams that kept him tossing and turning the night before. So vivid, so real…and all of them centered around the woman from the call at the barn the day before—all polka dots, wild hair and big doe eyes.

He frowned and shoved his casserole into the oven.

"Whoa." Brody rattled the front-page section of the *Bee* in his hands. "That nut job who keeps complaining about the parenting column wrote another letter to the editor, and this one's a doozy."

"Speaking of people who need to get a life." Wade rolled his eyes.

Sweat broke out on the back of Jack's neck. *Nut job, here. Present and accounted for.* "Who wants orange juice?"

He didn't wait for an answer, sloshing OJ into four glasses and plonking them down on the table purely in an attempt to avoid this next conversational land mine.

Was he proud of his latest missive? No, he was not. He'd gone too far when he'd called for the columnist's resignation. He wasn't out to get anyone fired, but come *on*. Parents didn't need to know what babies to follow on Instagram. They needed to know how to sleep train their six-month-old twins.

Hypothetically speaking, of course.

It's not hypothetical at all. The guys are right. You're losing it, my friend.

"The reporter's angry little pen pal says she should quit." Brody let out a whistle as he finished reading the letter to the editor, then passed it around the table for the others to peruse at their leisure.

Super.

"Did she?" Jack asked, shifting his weight from one foot to the other.

"Did she what?" Brody took a swig of his juice. "Quit?"

"Apparently not," Wade said, spreading open the paper's lifestyle section. "She's got a new column in here—'Five easy applesauce recipes for your infant or toddler.'"

Another listicle, like something that might be posted to Buzzfeed online. But hey, at least it was somewhat useful. And at least he wouldn't have a reporter's firing weighing on his conscience.

Thank God. He knew he needed to take it down a notch. He didn't use to be like this. He'd actually been a fun-loving guy at one point in time. A nice guy. A *decent* guy. Too decent, according to his ex. Maybe she'd find whatever she was looking for in San Francisco—a big life in the big city with a not-so-decent man and zero children.

Jack hoped so. He wanted her to be happy, because somewhere deep down he was still kind and decent. The past year had been a struggle, but he was coming out of the woods. Mostly.

"Do the twins like applesauce?" Wade said, folding the page with the parenting column into a neat square.

Jack raked a hand through his hair. "I honestly don't know. I've only recently begun letting them try something other than formula. They're pretty crazy about mashed bananas."

"Well, here. Maybe your mom could give one of the recipes a try." Wade offered the square of newsprint to Jack.

He was almost afraid to touch it, lest it burst into flames and give him away as the letter-writing nutjob. At least there was a fire extinguisher nearby.

"Thanks." Jack looked down at the words on the page and ran the pad of his thumb over the columnist's name, Queen Bee, clearly a nom de plume.

She could be anyone. She could have a Pulitzer for all he knew, but whoever she was, Jack was fairly certain she knew next to nothing about raising a child.

And that was absolutely none of his business. He didn't need to rely on his small-town newspaper for parenting advice. There was a pile of parenting books from the library stacked on his nightstand for that very purpose. He just hadn't come up with a spare minute to crack one of them open.

He wasn't sure why he'd made the irrational choice to channel all his frustration into complaining about Queen Bee's silly articles, but it needed to stop.

Probably.

No, definitely. It definitely needed to stop.

"Actually, I think I'll whip up some applesauce myself. My mom's doing enough." He tucked the article into the back pocket of his regulation Normex pants for safekeeping.

No way would he ask his mother to make his daughters homemade applesauce. She already insisted on taking care of the twins while he was on duty. The girls even had matching cribs in the room formerly known as his dad's man cave in the red brick house where Jack and his sister had grown up. He wasn't sure what he would have done without his family this past year, especially in the days right after Natalie had decided that motherhood "wasn't for her."

"Hey." Cap looked up from the sports page. "I know exactly what you need, Jack."

Please don't say a woman.

Jack sighed. Wasn't there a fire somewhere that needed putting out? Nothing major, just a small flame to get everyone's attention off him and onto something else. Preferably something that didn't involve Queen Bee and his letters to the editor.

"You need a night nanny." Cap shot him a triumphant grin.

"A what?" Jack said.

Cap shrugged. "A night nanny—someone to come in and take care of the girls at night while you sleep."

"Is that a thing?" Jack glanced around the table. Was he the only one who'd never heard of such a profession?

Brody nodded. "Oh, yeah. My brother and his wife got one of those when Susan went back to work. They said it was a lifesaver. She came over around ten at night and stayed until six in the morning."

Wade frowned. "I'm not sure I could sleep at night knowing there was a stranger lurking around my house."

Jack snorted. So not a problem. The entire population of Lovestruck could throw a party in his living room and he'd probably snooze through the entire thing.

"I'm telling you, a night nanny is the perfect solution. I can't believe I'm just now thinking of it." Cap sipped from his coffee cup, then peered into it when he realized it was empty.

Jack grabbed the pot from the coffeemaker on the kitchen counter and filled it for him. "Better late than never. I'll look into it."

Of course if Queen Bee had written a single column offering advice for new parents returning to work, he might have already gotten a night nanny. But no. Instead, his head was filled with useless information like the four cutest toddler shoes for fall and the top bathing suits for a summer in the baby pool.

At least he had a blueprint for applesauce in his back pocket. That was something.

Cap nodded. "Just wait. A night nanny will change your life."

Jack poured himself a steaming cup of Folgers breakfast blend—black, like his mood.

Change my life?

Maybe a night nanny wasn't such a bad idea.

Chapter Three

Dear Editor,

While I'm pleased to see Queen Bee, your parenting "expert," writing about practical matters, the first applesauce recipe in Tuesday's column was bitter to the point of being inedible. I've yet to attempt the other four recipes, but based on past experience with this columnist's work, I'm not holding my breath.

Sincerely,
Fired Up in Lovestruck

Madison maneuvered her grocery cart from the front entrance of Lovestruck's Village Market toward the produce section, nearly plowing down a tower of maple syrup jugs in the process. She needed to slow down. She knew this, but she was just so, so… *enraged*…that she couldn't help banging into a few things along the way.

Her pen pal had written yet another letter to the editor. Short and sweet this time and not quite as critical as the previous letters, but still. Couldn't Fired Up in Lovestruck tell she was trying?

Okay, so she hadn't exactly put each of the applesauce recipes to the test, but there hadn't been time to do so. The electricity in her apartment above the barn was still nonexistent. *Thank you, rural utilities services.* She'd been forced to sleep in Aunt Alice's guest room in the farmhouse the past two nights, and while her aunt genuinely didn't seem to mind, Madison hated to impose. She was also having a difficult time growing accustomed to her bedmate—Alice's rescue dog, Toby.

Madison generally loved dogs. If not for the strict no-pets policy in her apartment building in Manhattan, she'd have adopted one herself by now. Last year *Vogue* hired a delivery service to bring ten adoptable puppies to the office for Take Your Dog to Work Day, and she'd very nearly tucked a sweet long-haired

Chihuahua mix into her handbag and walked away with it, Elle Woods style.

Toby wasn't exactly an ordinary dog, though. He was Chinese crested—delicate, fine boned and, other than some wisps of fur on his ankles and the tip-top of his head, completely hairless. Madison hadn't gotten Alice to admit it yet, but she was fairly certain her aunt had adopted a hairless dog just so she could knit him sweaters. Toby's doggy closet runneth over. Madison was legitimately envious of his wardrobe. The poor naked thing was a bona fide fashionista, which may have been why he'd formed such a strong bond with her. It was as if he'd sensed a kindred spirit in Madison. When he wasn't at Main Street Yarn with Aunt Alice, he was curled into a ball in Madison's lap or hogging her pillow at bedtime. Honestly, the pup was a sweetheart, but he had an odd habit of burrowing beneath the bedsheets during the night. One of these days Madison would get used to her feet coming into contact with bare dog skin in the wee hours of the morning. She just hoped it happened sooner rather than later.

But Madison had bigger problems than hairless dogs and her dead flat iron at the moment. Mr. Grant didn't seem to mind Fired Up's latest letter much. It was short, sweet—sort of…at least compared to the previous letters—and to the point. But it bothered Madison more than any of the others had, probably because she'd actually believed in her applesauce column. It had seemed like just the sort of solid, hands-on advice that her readers wanted.

Correction: reader. Singular.

Plus, the quotation marks Fired Up had put around the word *expert* had really gotten to her. It was basically a troll's way of making those annoying air quotes that everybody hated. The fact that she wasn't actually an expert was beside the point. Fired Up didn't know a thing about her background. He didn't even know her real name.

She wasn't going to sit back and take the criticism this time. Enough was enough. Her job was at stake—not just her lame position at the *Lovestruck Bee*, but whatever glittering future awaited her back in Manhattan. Getting fired would put a huge dark stain on her résumé and make finding a new job in fashion journalism all the more impossible. She couldn't risk it. She was going to have to put that troll in his place, once and for all. All she needed was a bushelful of apples, a little quality time in Aunt Alice's kitchen and her laptop.

Lucky for her, Lovestruck was flush with apples this time of year. The town was dotted with orchards, and since late summer was peak tourist season, farmers made daily deliveries to the market. Apples of all varieties—Gala, Quinti, Ida Red, Jersey Mac—

spilled over the edges of bushel baskets piled in the center of the produce section.

Madison brought her grocery cart to an angry halt and reached for a rich, red piece of fruit, still warm from the summer sun. But just as her fingertips came into contact with the apple's shiny peel, someone plucked it out of her grasp.

Vermont still hated her, apparently, as did most of its inhabitants.

"Um, excuse me," she said to the apple thief's broad back.

Madison wasn't usually quite so confrontational. Not even in New York, where she'd once witnessed two grown men get into an actual brawl in the checkout line at CVS. But she'd had it with this place. She really had.

The man turned around, and she squared her shoulders, fully prepared to demand an apology. But he was awfully tall—tall enough that she had to tip her head back to get a good look at him, and as she did so, her gaze snagged on three red letters situated just above the pocket on his dark blue T-shirt.

LFD.

They seemed vaguely familiar, but Madison couldn't place them right away, probably because she was still in denial that she resided in *L* now instead of *NY*. A nagging sense of foreboding swept over her. Then the pectoral muscle beneath the letters flexed, and her mouth grew dry.

"Oh," the bearer of the rock-hard physique said.

He sounded less than pleased, which managed to snap Madison back to her senses long enough to meet his familiar steely gaze. Only one man in all of Vermont could possibly have eyes that blue paired with such a deep frown.

LFD.

Lovestruck Fire Department.

Of course.

"It's you," they both said simultaneously.

His gaze homed in on her mass of unruly curls, and the corner of his lips twitched. Madison had the sudden urge to grab an apple from her cart and conk him over his annoyingly handsome head.

She couldn't, obviously, because her cart was empty.

She lifted her chin. "You took my apple."

His gaze narrowed. "Pardon?"

"You *stole it* right out of my hand." Why had that sounded so much less crazy in her head?

"I assure you that wasn't my intention." He gestured toward the contents of his grocery cart. "Be my guest."

A dozen or more apples rolled around in the bottom of his basket. Madison couldn't have identified the apple in question if her life had depended on it.

Now was the time to back off and apologize. There were a million more apples in Vermont—hundreds, if not thousands, in this very store. It certainly didn't seem as if he'd intentionally plucked it from her hands.

But Madison didn't back down. She couldn't, because her life was a complete and total mess. And for some humiliating reason, Lieutenant Jack Cole seemed to have a front-row seat for her most embarrassing moments. Was clinging on to some tiny shred of pride really such a bad thing?

"Very well." She picked an apple at random and transferred it from his cart to hers.

"That's the one, huh? You sure?" His lips twitched again as if biting back a smile.

Sure, this *he smiles at.*

"I'm positive," she said. Why, oh why, had she chosen this hill to die on?

He nodded. "Okay, then."

"Okay," she echoed.

Then they both stood there, regarding each other for a beat. Madison desperately wanted to ask him why he needed so many apples. There wasn't a single other thing in his cart. Since he was wearing his Lovestruck Fire Department shirt, she figured this must be an official fireman grocery store run. But gosh, how much fruit did they go through down at the station? A lot, apparently, because he reached for

another from the bushel basket at the same moment
that Madison did, causing their hands to collide.

There it was again—that little zing of electricity
she'd felt the last time he'd touched her. Madison
couldn't move all of a sudden. She was paralyzed,
unable to do anything except blink up at the beautiful blue warmth of his irises. His gaze dropped to
her mouth, and her heart felt like it might beat right
out of her chest right there in the produce section.

But in a flash, his eyes met hers again. Icy blue,
this time. Stone cold.

A fresh wave of embarrassment washed over
her. Clearly, she'd been imagining things. Lieutenant Cole wasn't attracted to her in the slightest, and
that was *fine*. More than fine. She didn't even like
the man.

She took a giant backward step, eager to put some
space between them. But in her haste to get away,
she moved too fast, teetering on her red-soled stilettos—a holdover from her former, fashionable life.
Before she could right herself, she stumbled into a
row of bushel baskets. One basket tipped over, then
another…and another, sending apples careening everywhere and flying in all directions.

She scrambled after them at first, trying to scoop
them up and deposit as many as she could into her
cart. But the sheer number of them was staggering.

It was an apple avalanche, and there was nothing anyone could do to stop it.

Not even a card-carrying hero like Jack Cole.

Apples bounced around Jack's feet, falling faster than he could possibly catch them. He tried—oh, how he tried. He dove at them as they spilled onto the floor, but within seconds, Madison and Jack were both shin-deep in fruit.

She would have run away if she could, but a few hundred apples blocked the path to her getaway. *Super.*

Jack narrowed his gaze at her. "Pardon me for asking, but are you always this…"

Her face burned with heat as adjective after adjective spun round in her head, none of them flattering—*clumsy…ridiculous…*

Infatuated.

An apple must have hit her on the head and knocked a screw loose, because no way was she attracted to this man. He clearly brought out the very worst in her.

"Hostile?" he finally said.

"Hostile?" Her voice rose an octave or six, making her sound more like a cartoon character than a person, which seemed almost appropriate, given her current circumstances. Seriously though, if anyone was hostile around here, it was him. "I'll have you know that most people find me charming."

"Is that so?" He let out an unprecedented laugh, and a dimple flashed in his left cheek, because of course it did.

Dimple or not, the man was impossible. One minute he was glaring at her and the next, he was laughing at her. Except there'd been a sliver of a moment when he'd looked at her as if he'd wanted to kiss her. She was sure of it.

She lifted her chin. "Yes, it's absolutely so."

He said nothing. He just silently bent down, picked up one of the runaway apples and took a bite out of it while she stared at him in complete and utter confusion. What in the world was he doing?

The mind reeled.

Forbidden fruit, she thought, and for some strange reason, her heart started beating hard and fast again…so fast that she suddenly had trouble catching her breath.

Until a staticky voice rang out overhead, ending the magic spell once and for all.

"Clean up on aisle one!"

Three hours, four baking pans and a few batches of applesauce later, Madison sat across the kitchen table from her aunt Alice, poking her fork into another bite of warm apple crumble.

"This is delicious. I regret nothing," she said as cinnamon and sugar melted in her mouth.

"Nothing?" Her aunt lifted an amused brow as she meticulously covered one of several homemade apple pies with a sheet of nonstick aluminum foil. "Not a single thing?"

Madison had regrets. A few of them, to be honest. She most definitely regretted having to spend most of what was left in her paltry bank account on bruised apples, but she was trying her hardest to look on the bright side—at least she had pie.

So much pie!

It almost made interacting with Jack Cole worth the trouble. Emphasis on *almost*.

"This—" she waved a forkful of hot apple filling in Aunt Alice's direction "—is delicious. You're a goddess in the kitchen. That's all I'm saying."

"Well, we couldn't let all those apples go to waste now, could we?" Alice stood and added the foil-wrapped pie to the other three lined up on the butcher-block island in the center of the big farmhouse kitchen. Toby pranced at her feet, resplendent in a lacy knit sweater decorated with tiny crochet flowers.

Madison smiled. "Seriously, thank you. I've never made a pie before. It was fun."

She'd almost been in tears when she'd arrived back at Aunt Alice's big yellow house, with its crisp white trim and red brick chimney, carrying her half-dozen bags of sad apples. Moving to Vermont had been a mistake. It wasn't supposed to be this way. Things were supposed to be easier in Lovestruck. Gentler. She was supposed to have time to regroup here and breathe a little bit until the perfect job in fashion journalism came along, and instead, she'd been messing things up at every turn.

How was this possible? Wasn't small-town life supposed to be peaceful and idyllic?

The apple disaster had been the last straw, her rock bottom. But then Alice had taken one look at the contents of her grocery bags and suggested they bake a pie. Strangely enough, it was just what Madison needed. She'd had no idea how soothing baking could be. She liked the feel of the rolling pin in her hands and the predictability of knowing she could mix sugar and butter and flour and an hour later, end up with something sweet and delicious.

It made her believe in herself again, just the tiniest bit.

"Never?" Alice's hand stilled as she wiped down the countertop with a blue-and white-checked dishrag. She shook her head. "I'm sorry, dear. Of course you haven't. Your father…"

Madison held up a hand. "It's okay. I promise. Dad was great. He just wasn't much of a baker."

"You're right about that." Alice sighed. "At any rate, I'm glad I could teach you something new."

"Me, too." Madison stood to rinse her plate.

"And I'm glad you're here, even if the barn apartment didn't quite work out. You can stay as long as you like, dear. That's what family is for."

"Thank you." Madison smiled.

It wasn't the first time Alice had told her as much since she'd arrived from New York. Her aunt had repeated the sentiment every day, probably because every time she did, Madison reminded her the move was only temporary.

She didn't this time. It felt wrong tonight, somehow.

That's what family is for.

Was it? It had been a while since Madison herself had relied on family. She'd forgotten how nice it could feel to be part of a bigger whole.

"Actually, there's something else I might need help with." Madison ran a soapy sponge over her plate, focusing intently on the suds.

"Anything, dear." Aunt Alice scooped Toby into her arms, and he craned his neck to sniff at Madison's hair. She'd probably smell like apples for the rest of her life. "What is it this time? Peach pie? Blueberry?"

Madison wished her favor was pie related. Sadly, it was not. "My editor thinks I need to spend some time with children."

She'd been living on borrowed time since Mr. Grant had made the suggestion, but she couldn't keep putting it off with recipe columns. She was supposed to be the parenting expert, not a food columnist.

"Oh." Aunt Alice's brow furrowed. "What does he have in mind, exactly?"

"I honestly have no idea, but I have to come up with a plan. I hardly know any adults in Lovestruck, much less children." She glanced at Toby. Did three-year-old hairless dogs count? Doubtful.

Aunt Alice put him back down on the ground so she could flip through the wall calendar pinned to the refrigerator with a Vermont tourism magnet that said *I scream, you scream, we all scream for maple syrup*. She tapped her pointer finger on one of the weekend squares. "You could always volunteer at the library. They have story hour on Saturday afternoons."

"Really?" Madison brightened. An hour a week wasn't much, but it was something. "Do you think they'd let me do it?"

Alice patted her shoulder. "I can put in a good word for you."

"Perfect. Thank you."

Things were *finally* looking up.

Tomorrow's paper would be the turning point. Madison had sent an email to Mr. Grant an hour ago, and he'd already gotten back to her. Everything was already set into motion. Her run-in with Jack Cole at the market may have been her rock bottom, but she was already bouncing back.

No thanks to Lovestruck's finest.

"Although if you want some experience with infants, you could always come to the baby booties class I've got going on at the yarn shop." Alice shot her a hopeful glance.

Madison winced. "I don't know the first thing about knitting. Or crochet. I haven't picked up a skein of yarn since the last time I came to visit."

She felt terrible admitting as much. As a little girl, she'd loved spending time at Main Street Yarn, making basic knit hats on a plastic loom while Aunt Alice helped customers.

"You didn't know how to bake an apple pie until an hour ago." Her aunt shrugged.

Fair point. "Will there be babies there?"

"A few. But even better, there will be new moms. You might be able to line up a babysitting job."

It was worth a shot. At the very least, she could write a column or two about knitting baby items. "Count me in."

"Perfect!" Alice clapped her hands, and Toby let out three yips in rapid succession. "Class starts tomorrow night. I think this will be just what you need. No one needs more help than new moms do."

And then, just as Madison grabbed her laptop and headed off to the guest room, her aunt added with a snort. "Except maybe new dads."

Chapter Four

Dear Editor,

*This letter is in response to the recent corre-
spondence from Fired Up in Lovestruck regarding my column last Tuesday, "Five easy
applesauce recipes for your infant or toddler."
According to Fired Up, the first recipe listed
in the article was "bitter to the point of being
inedible."*

*Since Fired Up seems especially interested
in the accuracy of my column, might I make
a gentle suggestion? Followed correctly, the*

recipe yields a deliciously mild applesauce, perfect for babies. A common mistake when making applesauce is failing to remove all of the apple's seeds. This happens most often when using a food processor, which is understandable since cooking the apples with their skin is advisable in order to keep important nutrients as well as give your applesauce a nice, rosy color. Removing the seeds is quite important, though, because they are tannic. As a result, cooking them with the apples will leave the applesauce with a bitter flavor.

I would suggest that Fired Up try the recipe again. If my dear reader still considers the recipe too bitter, a dash of good old-fashioned Vermont maple syrup could be added. But if my suspicions are correct, Fired Up is the bitter one. Not my applesauce.

Sincerely,
Queen Bee

"What's all this?"

Wade's question startled Jack so much that he nearly hit his head on the inside of the refrigerator in the firehouse's kitchen where he was busy stacking Tupperware containers of homemade applesauce. Yesterday had been his day off, and when he hadn't been busy changing diapers or warming up bottles of formula, he'd been at the stove, trying to use up all the apples he'd purchased after the apple avalanche at the Village Market. Two tiny babies could only eat so much applesauce, though. And if fourteen years as a firefighter had taught him anything, it was that a group of guys stuck under one roof together for any period of time would eat just about anything.

"It's applesauce." Jack waved a Tupperware bowl in Wade's general direction. "Want some?"

"No, thanks. I just ate." Wade narrowed his gaze at the packed refrigerator shelves. "How much did you make? I thought you were trying out recipes for the girls. This looks like enough applesauce to feed an ar—"

Jack tensed as Wade's voice drifted off. He had the distinct feeling he was about to be busted in a major way. Couldn't a man make a few gallons of homemade applesauce without getting the third degree from his coworker?

Note to self: find some regular hobbies.

"Tell me this doesn't mean what I think it does." Wade shook his head. "My God, it does, doesn't it? *Fired Up* in Lovestruck. I can't believe I didn't see it until now."

"It's not a big deal." Jack slid a bowl and spoon across the counter toward Wade. Maybe if he could trick his friend into stuffing his face, they wouldn't have to talk to each other, and he could avoid this painful conversation altogether.

"It sure seems like one." Wade peeled the lid off the bowl and peered at its contents. "You've basically started an all-out war with a local reporter."

"Hardly." Jack swallowed. "It's more of a minor skirmish, *not* a war."

"Dude," Wade said around a mouthful of applesauce. "She wrote a letter to the editor *of her own newspaper* calling you bitter. Everyone in town is talking about it. That's not normal. *None of this* is normal."

He had a point. Still, Jack had actually felt relieved when he'd spotted her letter in the *Bee*. She'd called him out, and rightfully so. He'd definitely tossed the apples into his food processor, seeds and all. And now he had apples coming out of his ears—more than enough to experiment with, thanks to his recent flirtation in the produce department at the Village Market.

Thinking about it again, something hardened deep in his gut. He hadn't been *flirting*, or more accurately, if he had, it had been purely accidental. He had neither the time, nor the desire, for a woman in his life—especially a woman like the wild-haired beauty he kept bumping into.

Liar. You might not have the time, but the desire is another matter entirely.

Their fingertips had touched as they'd reached for the same apple, and *boom*. Jack had been hit with a longing so raw and so deep that he'd nearly kissed her right there in the produce section. It was insane. They didn't even know each other, and he was fairly certain she despised him.

Scratch that. She *definitely* despised him.

At least the new development in his ongoing feud with Queen Bee had helped keep his mind off his new crush. In the hours he'd spent making applesauce, he hadn't thought about her big doe eyes or bow-shaped lips more than a handful of times. Ten, tops.

Liar...again.

"You're not going to tell Cap, are you?" Jack said, gaze flitting in the direction of the apparatus bay where he'd last seen his boss inspecting one of the rigs.

Wade arched a brow. "Why not, since it's completely normal and healthy to be arguing with a woman you don't know via the local paper?"

Jack sighed.

"Fiiiine." Wade pointed his spoon at Jack. "But swear to me you're getting a night nanny. I have to believe all this nonsense is just temporary insanity brought on by single fatherhood and lack of sleep."

Jack raked a hand through his hair. "It's not as easy as it sounds. I called that service that Brody's sister recommended, and none of the résumés they emailed me were acceptable."

Maybe he was being overprotective, but nothing was more important than his girls. As much as he needed some help, he was having a hard time imagining letting a stranger take care of them. So far only Jack himself and other family members had watched over them.

Of course, that demographic included his ex-wife, and odds were, anyone the nanny service sent to him would probably be more interested in the twins than Natalie ever had been.

"Not a single one of them?" Wade tossed his spoon into the now-empty bowl with a clang. "I don't believe that for a minute. You've got to let go, man. Just a little bit."

Let go. It sounded so easy. So...*doable*. Except he'd been holding on so tightly to things for so long that relaxing his grip seemed impossible.

"I'll try," he conceded as he inserted a pod into the coffeemaker.

Wade brushed past him on the way to the refrigerator. "Nope. No trying. Either you hire the next applicant for the night nanny position, or I tell Cap about your secret identity."

"You're going to blackmail me into turning my children over to a complete stranger?" His head ached. There wasn't enough coffee in the world for this.

"A *competent* stranger," Wade countered. "Are you forgetting that you're going to be at home while he or she takes care of the girls? It's just part-time, while you sleep."

"I'm aware," Jack said, then took a long, fortifying sip from his coffee cup.

"Good. Either you hire the very next person who applies for the nanny job, or I'll tell everyone at the station about your cute little pseudonym." Wade slapped him on the back. "Don't worry. You'll thank me later. Deal?"

Jack nodded, only half paying attention, because his mind had begun to stray again. Apples tumbled through his thoughts and with them, a sublime ache. He'd forgotten what it felt like to be attracted to a woman, to wonder what it might be like to bury his hands in her hair and kiss her silly. He'd forgotten how good they smelled, especially *this* woman, like warm honey and apples…like home. He'd forgotten so damn much.

"Deal," he said absently.

Ready or not, Jack Cole was starting to remember.

Seeing her rebuttal letter printed in the paper gave Madison a definite thrill.

Take that, Fired Up.

Sure, it was an unconventional approach to dealing with the problem, but the *Lovestruck Bee* had only itself to blame. Its mandatary print-every-letter-to-the-editor policy had finally worked in her favor. She was practically skipping through the office when Mr. Grant tapped her on the shoulder and told her he needed to speak with her in his office.

Her stomach lurched. As much as she liked her boss, being called into his office was never a good thing.

"Yes, sir." She tightened her grip on her coffee cup as she followed him through the maze of desks toward his corner office overlooking Main Street.

Her mug was emblazoned with the words Busy Bee and featured a cartoon black-and-yellow honey-bee zipping around with a pair of oversize glasses on its little bee face. It was part of the office kitchen's collection of bee-themed coffee cups. The day before, she'd sipped her hazelnut blend from a mug that said Bee Happy. She hoped this morning's Busy Bee message was a sign she wasn't about to *bee* fired.

"Sit." Mr. Grant waved a hand toward the worn leather chair opposite his desk.

Madison took a deep breath and sat down.

"I'm going to be honest," her boss said, glancing out the window as he spoke. Across the street a few retirees were lined up in rocking chairs on the porch of the library. Farther down Madison could see the pristine brick exterior of the firehouse, Engine Co. 24.

Her gaze lingered on the fire truck parked out front, shiny and red, like a perfectly ripe apple. She wondered if Lieutenant Cole and his dreamy blue eyes were inside the building doing something heroic like sliding down a pole or walking around shirtless, covered in soot.

Or maybe he was off somewhere saving a kitten in a tree. Ugh, why did he have to be a firefighter? It made him infinitely hotter.

No pun intended.

Mr. Grant cleared his throat, dragging her attention back to the matter at hand—her possible imminent termination.

She squirmed in her chair. "Sorry. You were saying?"

"Right. Well." He folded his hands on the desk in front of him. "I'm sure you know why I wanted to speak with you."

The Busy Bee mug shook slightly in Madison's hands. Coffee sloshed dangerously close to the rim. "This is about my letter to the editor."

He shot finger guns at her. "Bingo."

Her stomach took another tumble, but at the same time she realized Mr. Grant was smiling. Why was he *smiling*?

Her boss wasn't exactly the smiley type, which meant this was either an uncommonly friendly firing or he actually had something positive to say.

"It was a brilliant idea," he said.

"It was?" Madison sat up a little straighter. "Right. I mean, it *was*."

"Positively brilliant." Mr. Grant's smile grew wider. "The phone's been ringing off the hook all day. My email in-box is full. Until this morning I didn't even realize such a thing could happen."

"Do you want me to help you clear it out?" she said, still unsure where exactly this meeting was headed.

"What? No." He shook his head. "I want you to keep it up."

She blinked. "Keep what up, exactly?"

"Keep arguing with Fired Up in Lovestruck in the letters-to-the-editor section. The readers are eating it up." He cupped a hand to his ear. "Do you hear that? It's the sound of phones ringing out front. You have fans now."

"Wow." Madison's throat clogged. She was fully aware this was just a small-town newspaper, not at all in the same league as a New York fashion magazine. But never once had she had this sort of praise heaped on her at *Vogue*.

It wasn't terrible. In fact, it felt sort of awesome. She was surprised at how much Mr. Grant's kind words meant to her. "I don't know what to say."

"You don't have to say anything at the moment, because I haven't gotten a new letter from Fired Up.

Hopefully, I will. And when that letter comes, I want you to respond again. Got it?"

Madison nodded. "Got it."

"Also, I still want you to spend some time with real-life kids. Your column needs to be good. Is that understood?" He jabbed his pointer finger onto the copy of the *Lovestruck Bee* spread open on his desk.

Madison was much more comfortable with this familiar, less effusive version of Mr. Grant. She nodded. "Absolutely. My aunt set me up with the library for story circle time on Saturday mornings, and tonight I'm attending knitting class in hopes of lining up a few babysitting gigs."

Her boss grunted. "I don't need the specifics. I just need you to turn in some good copy and keep arguing with Fired Up in Lovestruck."

She could do that, especially the second part. In fact, nothing would thrill her more. "Yes, sir."

Madison practically floated back to her desk, and she kept floating for the rest of the day, right up until it was time to walk next door for the baby booties class at Main Street Yarn.

"You look happy," Aunt Alice said as she gave Madison a hug and a kiss on the cheek.

"It's been a good day." Madison smiled. "A great day, actually."

"That's my girl." Alice winked, and Toby hopped off the crocheted dog bed tucked in the corner of the cash register area to scamper toward Madison and paw at her shins.

She scooped the tiny dog into her arms and looked around. The walls of the shop were all lined with cubby holes, each stacked with either skeins of yarn or yarn that had been wound into balls. From a distance, they almost looked like colored Easter eggs or crayons in a box. The cubby holes closest to the front of the store held yarn in delicate shades of white and ivory, which eventually switched to gentle pastel hues and ultimately, an explosion of vivid color near the back of the shop.

A large round table sat in the center of the sales floor, its beloved maple surface worn smooth with age. A ceramic bowl sat in the center of the table, piled high with balls of yarn in tints straight out of a baby shower—pale ballet pink, baby blue, minty green and a fair shade of yellow that reminded Madison of the fuzzy baby chicks she sometimes saw for sale at the Lovestruck Farmers' Market. Knitting patterns labeled Baby Booties for Beginners had been placed in front of the six chairs surrounding the table.

Back when she was a little girl, Madison typically spent a week of each summer vacation in Lovestruck with Aunt Alice. Her dad was usually too busy at work to tear himself from the office, so Alice would meet her at the train station and dote on her for the entire week as if Madison were her own. Aunt Alice had taught her how to make hats on a round loom at this very table.

The memory made Madison smile. In a way, her aunt had been the one to introduce her to fashion. She still had some of the hats she'd made on that loom, along with her sad, juvenile attempts at crocheted scarves.

"Do you remember how to cast on?" Alice said as she offered Madison a pair of slender, wooden knitting needles.

She placed Toby on the floor so he could resume his spot of honor on his crocheted dog bed and took the needles. They felt completely foreign in her grasp. "Not at all."

Alice winked. "No worries. This is a beginner class. You'll fit right in."

Her aunt was right...mostly. Two of Madison's classmates were regulars at Main Street Yarn who signed up for all of Alice's classes, regardless of skill level. The other three women who occupied seats alongside her at the old maple table were totally new to knitting. Two of them were in the late stages of pregnancy, both glowing as they struggled with a basic garter stitch. The third, situated right next to Madison, appeared to be around Aunt Alice's age and wore a cute pair of eyeglasses with cheerful red cat eye frames. She wondered if the older woman might be a grandmother, but didn't want to assume.

In any event, there wasn't an actual baby in sight. Madison tried to tamp down her disappointment as she fumbled with her knitting.

"I'm sorry," Aunt Alice mouthed to her at a quiet moment when all the other students had their heads bent over their booties in the making.

"It's fine," Madison mouthed back. "I'm having fun!"

She held up her tangle of pink yarn as evidence. In no way did the mess attached to her knitting needles resemble a tiny sock, but this was only the first night of the four-week-long class. Rome wasn't built in a day and all that.

Except Mr. Grant was expecting her to morph into Mary Poppins overnight, and for that, she needed to get her hands on some living, breathing babies—not just their shoes. She'd bought herself a little time with the buzz generated by her response to Fired Up, but who knew how long it would last? There was no guarantee her cranky correspondent would even write another letter to the editor.

Meanwhile, the only thing Madison had in common with Mary Poppins was an appreciation for polka dots. Seriously, Emily Blunt's wardrobe in the recent movie sequel had been amazing, but somehow Madison doubted she could get a workable column out of it. Oh, how she longed for her days at *Vogue*.

Once class was over, Madison straightened up the

shop, readying it for closing like she'd done when she was a little girl while Alice helped a few lingering students at the checkout area. The table was covered with bits of yarn and practice rows stitched together in pastel colors. But as Madison picked through the discarded items, she found a tiny toe-shaped tip of a baby bootie still attached to a slender bamboo knitting needle. It was crafted from pale, peachy-pink yarn—the same yarn her knitting neighbor to her right had been using during class.

She looked up, hoping to catch a glimpse of the woman with the red cat-eye glasses, but she wasn't among the small crowd gathered near the register.

Uh-oh.

Aunt Alice had assigned them all homework, and if the knitter didn't get ten new rows added to her project, she'd never be able to catch up during the next class. Madison grabbed the knitting needle and the ball of yarn it was attached to and hurried to the front of the shop.

"Knitting emergency!" She dashed past her aunt, waving the needles in explanation as she pushed through the shop's front door. "I'll be right back."

She caught sight of the cute cat-eye glasses just a few feet away, where the woman was about to climb into the driver's seat of a boxy little minivan.

"Wait!" Madison called out. "You forgot something."

She caught up to her fellow student just in time.

The woman pressed a hand to her heart when she spotted her creation in Madison's grasp. "Oh, my. I can't believe I left that behind! Thank you so much."

"No problem. I'm glad I caught up to you." Madison handed her the bundle of knitting. "I'm Madison, by the way."

"Thanks again, Madison. I'm Sarah." The older woman smiled, and as she bent to tuck the yarn and needles into her bag, Madison caught sight of two infant car seats tucked neatly into the backseat of Sarah's minivan.

She gasped. Now what, though?

Nice to meet you, Sarah. Can I borrow your babies?

Sarah let out a laugh. "My husband is home alone with our two granddaughters. They're only six months old, so I thought I'd rush home in case he needed rescuing."

Correction: Can I borrow your grandbabies?

Madison cleared her throat. "Wow, twins."

"Yes, they're precious. Honestly, they're both the sweetest little angels. But twins can be a handful, so we try and help out when we can." Sarah nodded and gave a tiny shrug as if Madison knew precisely how much of a handful a pair of angelic twin baby girls could be.

She didn't, obviously. She had no clue whatsoever. If she'd had any idea at all, she never would have blurted out the words that followed. "They sound adorable. Let me know if you ever need a babysitter. I'd...um...love to help out sometime."

Sarah peered at Madison over her cat-eye frames. "Really?"

"Really." Madison nodded. If she could handle one baby, surely she could handle two.

How much harder could it be?

Warning bells sounded in the back of her head, reminding Madison that she'd never in her life changed a single diaper, much less two at a time.

"Well, well, Madison. You just might be the answer to all our prayers." Sarah beamed.

I highly doubt it. And yet, Madison pasted on a smile. She'd worked for the toughest editor on Madison Avenue and lived to tell about it. She could survive a few hours with twin six-month-olds. Her career—as pathetic as it was at the moment—depended on it.

"It just so happens my son, John, is looking to hire a part-time night nanny. The mother isn't...well, let's just say she's no longer in the picture." Sarah looked Madison up and down. "I have a feeling the two of you should meet. The sooner, the better."

Chapter Five

Dear Editor,

My sincerest apologies to Queen Bee for my comments about the applesauce recipes recently listed in her column. Upon further experimentation, I concede that her advice about removing the apple seeds was entirely correct.

However, in today's paper readers are treated to yet another whimsical dribble of words from Queen Bee. While "Three Ways to Use Yarn to Entertain Your Toddler" seems helpful on the surface, I must ask why a profes-

sional journalist insists on writing her mate-
rial in this annoying list format. Also, a mere
three items hardly constitute a list.

　　Three? Seriously?

Sincerely,
Fired Up in Lovestruck

*T*he sooner, the better.

They'd been Sarah Cole's exact words when she'd called Jack at the station the night before.

Her name is Madison Jules, and I think she's just what you're looking for.

Jack sighed as he ran a hand over Ella's soft, downy head and glanced out the window of the Lovestruck Bean. His mom had been insistent—he was to call the woman she'd met at her knitting class immediately for an interview.

In theory, Jack agreed. In practice, however, an immediate interview necessitated getting a substitute for the second day of his shift. He'd done so, mainly because he was well aware of how indebted he was to his mom. There was absolutely no room for negotiation. If she wanted him to do something, he did it. Plus, the guys at the firehouse were more than happy to cover for him if it meant he might get some actual help at home. He hadn't even had to secure a sub. Wade volunteered to do it for him, so long as Jack stuck by his earlier promise to hire the next qualified applicant for the job.

So Jack had acquiesced and made the call. A few hours of phone tag with the mystery woman in question had followed, but he'd eventually scheduled an interview via text. Then he'd headed home early, tucked Ella and Emma into their baby wrap carrier and trudged down to the coffee shop to meet his possible future night nanny. And now...

Now she was late, which didn't exactly bode well.

He rocked back and forth, keeping up the gentle motion that typically lulled the twins to sleep. It wasn't quite working, though. Emma cooed happily, and her tiny little eyelashes were doing the slow-blink thing that meant a nap was imminent, but Ella's little legs kicked up a storm.

"Shh," he murmured and paced the length of the coffee shop. Maybe he should have had the nanny come to the house instead of trying to do this over maple macchiatos in one of the busiest places on Main Street.

Then again, he'd never set eyes on Madison Jules. He didn't know the first thing about the woman, other than she liked to knit baby booties. That seemed like an excellent sign, though. It conjured an image in Jack's head of a grandmother-type with her hair in a bun and glasses hanging from a chain around her neck. Someone whose entire life revolved around babies. Someone punctual.

He frowned and dug his phone out of his pocket to check the time. A text message flashed on the display.

Running a few minutes late. So sorry. Almost there.

The message was followed by two emojis—matching cartoon baby heads.

Jack stopped pacing.

Emojis?

He glanced out the window again, somehow no longer certain his night nanny was an actual grandmother. But that was fine, wasn't it? Shame on him, really, for jumping to conclusions about knitters.

Everything's going to be fine.

Ella let out a happy squeal, rousing a sleepy-eyed Emma. Jack pressed a soft kiss to the tops of their sweet little heads. First one, then the other. Then he looked back up and froze when his gaze locked on a familiar woman dashing through the crosswalk, straight toward him.

She had a halo of dark, windswept curls and warm, brown eyes—eyes that he'd seen in his dreams for several nights running. She was wearing another pair of sky-high stilettos with glossy red soles that were ridiculously impractical for rural Vermont, but damned if they didn't make her legs look a million miles long. A large designer handbag was slung over one of her slender shoulders, perfect for carrying around a bushelful of apples.

Or, Jack thought nonsensically, possibly his heart.

His jaw clenched as once again, his mother's words spun through his head.

Her name is Madison Jules...
She's just what you're looking for.

Madison was running late, and it was all Fired Up's fault.

She'd planned her entire lunch hour around the coffee date she'd scheduled with Sarah's son, John, but then Mr. Grant had called her into his office—again—to gush about the ongoing success of the feud. She'd been forced to sit and pretend to be excited about the fact that some random stranger was publicly insulting her again, as if it was a good thing.

It *was* a good thing, she supposed. Under the current circumstances, anyway. So long as she and Fired Up kept antagonizing each other, her job was secure.

But being mocked over and over didn't exactly feel great. She wanted to be appreciated for her actual work, not the fact that she'd managed to spectacularly antagonize one of her readers. Was that really too much to ask?

A pickup truck honked at her as she dashed

through the crosswalk. She waved in apology and blew a corkscrew lock of hair out of her face. She was *so late*. There was no way she'd get the night nanny job. Maybe that was okay, because she wasn't sure she even wanted it. She should be in Manhattan right now, pitching articles for Fashion Week. Instead, her boss had decided to print her troll's recent letter to the editor on the *front page*.

Oh, how the mighty—and stylish—had fallen.

The minute her nanny interview was over, she needed to send another round of emails to her contacts in New York. She needed to get out of Lovestruck. She needed her life back—her *real* life.

But first she needed to convince Sarah's son that she was the next best thing to Mrs. Doubtfire. She was *so* not in the mood for this.

"Sorry!" she called out to anyone and everyone as she burst through the door of the Lovestruck Bean.

Every head in the establishment swiveled in her direction, save one. There didn't seem to be an infant in sight, much less twins, and within seconds the patrons all turned their attention back to their coffee drinks.

Madison deflated a little, and then narrowed her gaze at the broad, muscled back of the person who'd managed to ignore her frazzled arrival. Heat crawled up her neck, and her stomach did a nervous little flip. She'd know that back anywhere.

Ugh, what was the surly firefighter doing here? This wasn't good. Not good at all, given her track record of making a complete idiot out of herself every time he was near.

She squared her shoulders. *Fine.* She'd deal with it. Sarah's son hadn't even arrived yet, anyway. Maybe Lieutenant Grumpy would be gone by then. He definitely didn't seem like the type to linger over his latte.

She fished through her bag for her cell phone and fired off another text to John, the father of Sarah's angelic grandtwins, just to let him know she was at the Bean, ready and waiting. The second she hit Send, a nearby phone chimed with an incoming text message.

Odd. Madison gnawed on her bottom lip and glanced around. She tried to ignore Lieutenant Cole, but as usual, her attention was drawn to him like a magnet. So very annoying.

She frowned as she watched him pull an iPhone out of his back pocket. *No.* Her pulse kicked up a notch as she checked her own phone, and sure enough, a read receipt flashed beneath the text she'd just sent.

No.

Way.

He couldn't possibly be Sarah's son, could he? Madison hadn't caught Sarah's last name. She only knew that the single dad in need of a night nanny was named John.

Her heart sank to the soles of her patent leather Louboutin stilettos. Jack was a nickname for John, wasn't it? She cursed small-town life under her breath. This would never happen in a city as big as Manhattan. In New York, she could have humiliated herself in the produce section of the supermarket and taken solace in the fact that she'd never again run into the hot first responder who'd witnessed her mortification.

Flight-or-fight instinct kicked in hard, and she started toward the door. She couldn't work for *him*. No way, no how. She wasn't sure if she despised him or if she wanted him to kiss her, and neither of those options was appropriate for an employer-employee relationship.

But her feet slowed to a stop halfway to the exit as the full implication of the sight of his chiseled back finally dawned on her. Jack had seen her text. He'd probably seen her approaching the coffee shop. Yet, there he stood—actively avoiding her.

Message received. He didn't want to hire her any more than she wanted to be his nanny. It shouldn't have bothered her, considering the fact that she was midflight herself. But it *did* bother her. Very, very much.

She spun around, marched straight over to him and tapped him on his sculpted shoulder. Good grief, how often did someone have to work out to have muscles like that?

She contemplated this question as he slowly turned to face her, mainly so she wouldn't be forced to think about why she always seemed to be poking him in order to instigate a confrontation. But then there he was—looking down at her from his towering height—and she suddenly couldn't think at all. Or breathe. Or do much of anything other than gape at the sight of him with two small babies strapped to his chest in some kind of sling contraption.

Her throat went dry. She wasn't even a baby person, but wow. This was beyond adorable. He couldn't have looked more attractive if he'd been caught saving an entire family of kittens from a tree.

"Hello," he said, frowning. As usual.

Madison felt herself smile as she took in the pink bow headbands jauntily placed on each of the babies' heads. Twin girls—identical, with matching, precious faces, tiny rosebud mouths and their father's dreamy blue eyes. One of them laughed and kicked her little feet, and it took every bit of self-control Madison possessed not to melt into a gooey puddle at Jack Cole's arrogant feet.

She forced herself to meet his gaze. "Are you *hiding* from me?"

"No," he lied, the twitch in his scowl a dead giveaway.

Madison crossed her arms. "So you normally skulk in corners like this?"

"Always. I'm an expert skulker." He shrugged one massive shoulder. "It's kind of my thing."

She smiled again before she could stop herself. "We keep…um…running into each other, but it seems we haven't met properly. I'm Madison Jules."

She stuck out her hand, and he took it. She braced herself for another delicious spark like she'd experienced the other brief moments they'd touched, but this time was different. His grasp was warm, and there was something more honest about it this time. Tender, almost.

It made Madison feel oddly weepy. She aimed her attention back toward one of the twins, blinking at her with impossibly long eyelashes. Were all babies this cute, or just his?

"So." She swallowed. "You have twins."

"I do." He dipped his chin toward one of the girls and then the other. "Emma and Ella."

Even their names were darling.

Madison nodded. "I met your mom last night at knitting class and she told me you were looking for a night nanny."

Why was she still talking? She was supposed to chastise him for hiding from her and then walk away with her dignity intact instead of hinting that she might be serious about the job.

He rested a protective hand on each of his daughters' tiny chests. "Right, but…"

"But you think I'd be terrible at it?" She would, probably. But the fact that he thought so stung for reasons she didn't care to contemplate.

"I didn't say that," he countered.

"You didn't have to."

He shook his head. "It's not…"

Then he stopped, sighed and glanced out the window toward the fire station across the street. The air between them swirled with the heady, homey scents of sweet maple and freshly ground coffee. Madison couldn't help but wonder what it would be like to rock this man's beautiful babies in her arms, to feed them and dress them in warm footy pajamas and press tender kisses to their soft little heads while their daddy slept in the next room.

The notion was ridiculously intoxicating. God, what was happening to her?

"Look, I know I haven't made the best first impression. Maybe we could start over? I'm sorry I'm late for this interview, but I got distracted this morning by…" She glanced down at the copy of the *Bee* in her hand and tossed it onto a nearby table. Facedown, so she wouldn't have to see Fired Up's latest missive in the corner of the front page. "Never mind. It's dumb."

So dumb.

Three bullet points totally counted as a list. What could someone who wrote handwritten snail mail possibly know about modern journalism? Absolutely nothing. Readers had the attention span of gnats nowadays. If she didn't organize her articles into tiny, easily digestible bites, no one would read them. It was just the way thing were.

But why she was wasting her time thinking about Fired Up while she was in the throes of the most awkward job interview of all time was a mystery she couldn't begin to fathom.

"*Anyway.* I might not be the worst person in the world to babysit your twins." Her heart gave a wistful little squeeze. *Don't say it, just don't.* "I grew up without a mom around, too, so…"

His gaze swiveled back toward her, and his icy blue eyes softened, ever so slightly. Madison felt achingly exposed all of a sudden, so she hugged her Louis Vuitton tote to her chest like a child with a security blanket.

"Right. Well," she stammered. "Good luck finding the perfect nanny."

"Wait," he snapped as she turned to go. Then softer, almost under his breath, he said. "Just wait a minute. Please?"

Every logical thought in her head told her to walk away and never look back, but Madison had never been a slave to logic. It was probably the most striking difference between her and her nemesis, Fired

Up. So she stopped, took a deep breath and waited for whatever it was that Jack Cole wanted to say.

"Are you at all—" His gaze narrowed and he enunciated the following word with great care "—*qualified*?"

Not in the slightest. Madison's only response was a hopeful smile.

He gave it another shot. "Have watched over a little one before? *Ever?*"

"There's a three-year-old named Toby who positively adores me," she said proudly.

It wasn't a lie. Not entirely. He'd said *little one*, and Toby was definitely little, albeit not exactly human.

"Okay, then. I suppose you're hired." Jack Cole nodded, and an irrational surge of joy flowed through Madison until her hands started to shake. "Can you start tonight?"

Tonight? As in, just a few hours from now?

"Absolutely." She nodded with far too much enthusiasm for a person who didn't actually want the job in question.

And it was then that Madison realized she wasn't entirely sure what—or more accurately, who—she wanted anymore.

Madison arrived at Jack's house promptly at six, anxious to show that yes, she was an actual, responsible adult who could get places on time when she wasn't feeling hopelessly distracted by a letter-writing troll with no sense of humor or whimsy whatsoever. Unfortunately, this stunning show of punctuality meant that she'd had to go straight to her new night nanny gig from her job at the paper, so she was still dressed in her best Chanel blouse and Marc Jacobs skirt with the twirly hem, along with her go-to pair of Louboutin heels. Not exactly prime nanny attire, but she'd have to make it work. They were babies. How much harm could they do?

She knocked on the door, reminding herself not to go all breathless when Jack answered. He was her boss now. Not her *real* boss, technically, since this was more of an undercover situation than her actual career. But still, boundaries and all that.

Not to mention the fact that she still found him wholly annoying. Why shouldn't she? He thought she'd be such a terrible nanny that he'd actively hid from her at the Bean. Never mind that his instincts had probably been spot-on, hiding from her was just mean and, truth be told, par for the course for the cranky fireman.

There was nothing annoying about his appearance when the door swung open, though. He was wearing a T-shirt that perfectly hugged his firefighting biceps and a pair of faded jeans that looked as soft and comfy as something straight out of a dryer sheet commercial. They were the exact same shade of blue as his eyes, which yes, could have been construed as *mildly* annoying if Madison had been in any way attracted to his cozy, single-dad vibe. But she wasn't.

Not much, anyway.

"Hi," she said. "Night nanny reporting for duty."

He looked up her and down, and a slight frown tugged at the corner of his mouth as his gaze lingered on her shimmery pink blouse. "Um, is that what you're wearing?"

She arched a brow. "Do you have something against French fashion?"

"No. It's just…" His frown deepened. Honestly, she'd never met such a frowny man in her life. "Never mind."

Good. She didn't want to get into another argument with him before she even managed to breach the perimeter of his home. "Shall I come inside now?"

"Oh." He cleared his throat. "Of course. Sure."

Madison stepped inside as he swung the door open wide with about as much enthusiasm as someone welcoming the plague into his home. Things were going great so far. Just peachy.

She looked around and was surprised to find his cottage warm and inviting—in direct opposition to Lieutenant Cole's general mood pretty much every time she'd been around him—and she couldn't help but wonder if he was usually a kinder, gentler version of himself and for some reason saved his grumpier moments just for her. She was beginning to suspect the latter, which intrigued her more than she wanted to admit.

Focus.

Babies. Column. Professionalism.

She squared her shoulders and did her best to give off a Mary Poppins vibe. "Where are the twins?"

"Their room is right down the hall." Jack led the way, and she walked alongside him, doing her best to ignore the way his heroic muscles flexed as he moved.

For about the thousandth time, Madison wished he was an accountant or an engineer instead of a fireman. Honestly, anything that didn't involve saving innocent people from burning buildings or spending an ounce of time in the gym.

"Here we are." He pushed a door open, revealing a cotton-candy-hued nursery that made her melt right there on the spot.

It was as pink and girly as a cupcake. She loved every inch of it.

"Please tell me you painted these walls yourself," she said before she could stop the flow of nonsense from her mouth.

"I did, why?"

"No reason," she said, biting down hard on her lip

to keep herself from smiling at the thought of Jack
with baby-pink paint spatters in his hair. *Adorable.*

A squealing sound came from one of the pretty
white cribs that sat side by side against the far wall.
Baby sounds—right, the whole reason she was here.

She walked over to the crib and peered down at
the sweet infant lying on her back and playing with
her feet, much like the happy baby pose Madison
had done about a thousand times in yoga. She'd had
no idea how on the nose those pose names could be.

"Why, hello there, Emma," she said in her gentlest tone.

"That's Ella," Jack corrected.

"Totally." Madison nodded. "Ella is what I meant
to say."

Good grief, she couldn't even tell them apart.

Her grip on the edge of the crib tightened as the
first wave of panic washed over her. What was she
doing here? Was Jack really going to just stand there
and watch her do her job? He was supposed to be
sleeping.

She smiled at him. *Go to bed. Please, please just
go to sleep.*

He didn't budge. He just stood there as if he was
waiting for something, and that something probably
had to do with her actually interacting with one of
his children.

Okay, then. She was going to have to pick Ella up.

No problem. She could totally do that. She'd never actually held a baby before, but how hard could it be? It was probably no different than holding Toby, especially since Toby didn't even have fur.

"Here we go," she murmured, reaching into the crib. "Come here, Emma sweetheart."

"Ella," Jack said.

Not helping! Madison slid her hands beneath Ella's tiny back, but trying to actually lift her felt strangely similar to trying to scoop up a wet, floppy noodle.

Not that Madison knew much about noodles, either, since apparently, she was a complete failure in the domestic realm. Gosh, why hadn't she ever taken home ec or child development in high school?

Because you were too busy perfecting your stay-stitching and hemming techniques in sewing class and writing about Fashion Week for the school paper.

She'd nailed her final senior sewing project—a white faux fur swing coat. She'd actually worn it last winter to the *Vogue* offices and gotten loads of compliments.

The baby in her hands kicked, drawing her back to the present…to Vermont, where she was an utter failure at everything that mattered.

"It's okay, baby. I've got you." Time was ticking away, and she'd yet to heave the sweet little tot into her arms. She was going to have to just do it and hope for the best before Jack realized what a mistake he'd made and told her to leave.

As carefully as possible, she picked Ella up, being especially mindful of her soft baby head, because she remembered reading something about that once in a magazine. It was awkward at first, because Ella insisted on squirming instead of just peering up at her and waiting patiently to be lifted, like Toby always did. But nor did she try to lick Madison's face—Toby's favorite thing—and that seemed like a definite bonus.

Finally, she managed to get Ella snuggled against her chest and was rewarded with a breathy little coo that gave her heartstrings a wholly unexpected tug. *I did it!* She breathed a sigh of relief. Hanging out with these two cuties wouldn't be so hard. Five minutes down, seven hours and fifty-five minutes to go.

She snuck a glance at Jack, who seemed to be watching her with far less open hostility than he normally did. In fact, there was an aching quality to the way he was looking at her. It made her heart beat hard, and she almost forgot that at some point she'd have to pick up *both* of his daughters at the same time. Was that even possible? She wasn't an octopus.

"There, there," she whispered when the baby in her arms whimpered. "I've got you, Emma."

"Ella." Jack sighed and the tender expression on his face faded away.

Madison breathed the tiniest bit easier. She could handle a distant Jack Cole. The gentle, scruffy, single-dad version of him was shockingly appealing all of a sudden.

"I knew that," she lied. "I was just testing you."

What had she gotten herself into?

What have I done?

Jack stared at his bedroom ceiling, wide awake at three in the morning. Madison's presence in his home was impossible to ignore. Somewhere beyond his closed bedroom door, he could hear the lilting softness of her voice as she talked to Emma and Ella in hushed tones. He pictured her delicate feet tiptoeing from one end of the house to the other every time one of his cedar floorboards creaked. Every move she made seemed to echo with sound that vibrated through him, setting his senses on fire.

He knew it was only his imagination. To Madison's credit, she wasn't actually making much noise. The twins were having a good night. Every time Ella or Emma starting crying, the tears seemed to stop within seconds. That was when the rhythmic sound of the rocking chair would start, lulling him to sleep right along with his daughters.

But inevitably, he'd dream about Madison and

wake up minutes later in a tangle of bedsheets, gasping for air.

This was never going to work. The whole reason for hiring a night nanny was so he could get some rest, and simply breathing the same air as Madison made him feel distinctly *restless*.

He hadn't had a choice in the matter, though. He'd promised Wade he would hire the next qualified applicant. Madison had been pretty vague about her experience, and Jack hadn't asked a single question about the child she'd mentioned—Toby—who "positively adored" her. Why wouldn't he? She seemed perfectly worthy of adoration.

Besides, Jack had already made up his mind to hire her at that point. Not at first, obviously. At first, he'd been more than a little skeptical. And yeah, he'd actually been hiding from her in hopes of avoiding ending up with a nanny who seemed to court chaos wherever she went.

It was the comment about growing up without a mother that had done him in. Not just the words, but the way she'd said them—so matter-of-factly, even though he could see how vulnerable and open they'd made her feel. Madison was a mystery he couldn't begin to unravel, but in that moment of truth, he'd wondered if maybe his mother had been right. Maybe she really was just what he was looking for—not for him, but for Ella and Emma. Maybe she could care for his girls and understand them in a way that no one else could.

He hoped so. God, how he hoped. They deserved more than just a single father who worried every damn day that he'd never be enough for them. He wanted to be the rock his daughters needed more than anything else in the world, but he was just one person. What if something happened to him at work one day? He was a firefighter. He put his life on the line on the regular without thinking twice about it. It was his duty.

He squeezed his eyes shut tight and pressed the heels of his hands against his eyelids until he saw spots. One day at a time, he reminded himself. He just had to do his best, take each day as it came and have faith it would all work out. Hiring Madison didn't make much sense on the surface, but it felt right. For an honest, aching moment in the coffee shop, it had even felt like destiny.

Now, here in the dark, it felt like a mistake. Had he lost his mind? Just days ago, Madison had almost burned down a barn with a hairstyling tool and now he'd given her free rein over his oven, his stove, his microwave and probably a dozen or so highly flammable household goods. She didn't even seem to know how to dress appropriately for taking care of infants. The thought of her dry-cleaning bill was enough to give him a migraine.

And she'd looked a little panicky before she'd picked up Emma. *Ella, damn it! Now she's got you mixing them up.* But once his baby had been in her arms, Madison's whole body seemed to sigh, and Jack had never wanted to kiss a woman so badly in his life.

He threw the duvet aside and climbed out of bed. Once he took a quick look around to make sure everything was safe and sound, maybe he'd be able to sleep. He'd act like he needed a glass of water or something. Nothing out of the ordinary about that, right?

Sure. Because the only thing keeping you awake at night is fire safety. It has nothing at all to do with the fact that you'd walk through a burning building just to kiss the woman who's puttering around your house while you lie in bed alone.

His teeth clenched as he pulled a T-shirt over his head and tugged it into place. After days, weeks and *months* of rigidly controlling everything around him, he'd allowed himself to become the oldest and worst sort of cliché—a dad who was hopelessly attracted to the nanny. He wondered what Queen Bee would have to say about this most inconvenient turn of events.

A lot, probably.

In fairness, he'd been attracted to Madison *before* she'd become the nanny. He didn't really understand it. He'd gone months without thinking about any sort of physical intimacy at all, and then just the brush of Madison's fingertips had nearly dragged him to his knees. It defied logic. He *ached* for her.

He desperately wished he didn't—then, and especially now. If forced to justify his predicament to Queen Bee, he would have said it didn't really matter if he found his nanny attractive because nothing would come of it. Ever. His family came first, followed by his job. There was nothing left of him after that—not even enough for a brief physical encounter and certainly not enough for a relationship. That was the sad truth of the matter.

Queen Bee would probably roll her eyes and call him a liar, not that he had much stock in her opinion. Still, the thought was infuriating.

He slammed the dresser drawer shut and stalked out of the bedroom. The hallway was dark, and even though he'd been moving about the shadows of his home every single night since the twins had been born—six months of late-night feedings, six months of midnight diaper changes and bottle washing—he stubbed his toe on the baseboard as if he'd suddenly wandered into the unknown. Lost.

He cursed under his breath and limped toward the kitchen, blinking against the assault from the overhead light in the den. Something seemed off. The room was empty. Madison and the girls were nowhere to be seen, but it looked like a baby powder bomb had gone off. Just about every surface was covered with a thin layer of the stuff.

Jack sneezed three times in rapid succession. Then he shook his head in an attempt to rattle his sinuses free and sneezed again. Once he was able to fully breathe, he took a closer look at the mess. Half a dozen diapers littered the floor. Weirdly, they seemed clean. They were just sort of…mangled? Most of the self-adhesive strips were doubled over and stuck to themselves. Jack stared down at the mess and shook his head.

Clearly, Madison had never changed a diaper before. He knew the signs well. Been there, done that, got the T-shirt. There was one very important difference between his situation and Madison's, though. Jack had never insisted he'd make a great night nanny.

A darkened iPad had been abandoned in the middle of the diaper debris. He bent to pick to up, dusted the baby powder from its screen and pressed the home button. A diagram with directions for mixing baby cereal flashed to life. Jack sighed. He was almost afraid of whatever disaster awaited him in the kitchen.

Rightly so, as it turned out. The sink was full of half-empty bottles, the microwave door was open and a bowl with the hardened remains of rice cereal sat on the rotating tray. Of course. Where Madison

Jules went, disaster followed. Why would he have expected anything less?

Jack pinched the bridge of his nose. He was going to have to fire her. He didn't have much of a choice, did he? The mess didn't matter, but the implications of it most definitely did. She'd clearly never been anyone's nanny. He'd bet good money on the notion that she'd never babysat anyone before, either.

This is what he got for thinking with his heart instead of his head and going all tender inside at the thought of Madison as a motherless little girl. Had he learned nothing from the Natalie fiasco? His heart couldn't be trusted. It got him in trouble every time.

Not qualified.

Not qualified *at all.*

He was off the hook. He could go back down the hall where she was probably creating more mayhem in the twins' bedroom and fire her right that second. Even Wade would have done the same.

For some reason he wasn't in much of a hurry to do so. Instead, he flipped on the faucet and let the water get steaming hot. Then he went to work, washing bottles and putting them in the electric steamer, any hope of getting a proper night's sleep lost, once and for all.

Once the kitchen was put back together, he tackled the den. Half an hour later he had baby powder in personal places he hadn't even realized he possessed, but his home was somewhat orderly. He took out the trash, picked up Madison's iPad and walked with purpose toward the nursery. He'd simply hand her the tablet and let her go. Surely, she'd understand. On some level, she'd probably even be relieved.

Or, she'd hate him even more. Either way, he was doing the right thing. No question.

But his footsteps slowed as his daughters' bedroom came into view. A faint sliver of light was visible beneath the closed door, and he waited for a long moment with his hand on the doorknob, straining to hear Madison's voice or the quiet swish of the gliding rocking chair. He heard nothing, just the hushed fury of his own heart, pounding in his chest. Too fast. Too hard.

He turned the knob as slowly and quietly as he could, then gave the door a gentle push. It opened with a muffled groan, and a thick lump formed in his throat at the sight of what he found inside.

Madison was fast asleep in the glider with a twin tucked into the crook of each elbow, his babies pressed snugly against her soft curves. Ella and Emma were dressed in their fanciest set of matching pajamas—ultrasoft white onesies scattered with tiny pink rosebuds and a profusion of pink satin ruffles. Their names were spelled out in swirling embroidery on their tiny chests, and even though Jack suspected

Madison had dressed Ella in Emma's pajamas and vice versa, he couldn't quite bring himself to care.

He'd made the same mistake on more than one occasion, and it hardly seemed like something to complain about because his girls looked perfectly content, perfectly happy. Moonlight poured in through the big picture window, bathing their sweet faces in silvery light. Ella's fist wrapped tight around one of Madison's slender fingers, and Emma made the snuffling little lamb noises that she only made when she was in her very best mood.

This. Jack swallowed hard. *This is what matters most.*

Not the baby powder explosion, not the mess, not even the learning curve. Connection mattered. Love mattered. And if there was even the possibility that his daughters might find that with Madison, who was he to take it away?

He opened the YouTube browser on the iPad, clicked on a medley of lullabies and placed the tablet gently on the table beside the glider. He studied Madison's features—so damned beautiful, like something out of a dream in the lavender light of the full moon. *Who are you?* he wondered. *Who are you, really?* What strange twist of fate had brought him such an inexperienced nanny, and why did he want so badly for her to stay?

It was late, and he was suddenly tired again.

Maybe more tired than he'd ever been, so he snuck out of the room and walked the quiet, lonely path back toward his bed.

And for the first night in a very long time, Jack Cole slept like a baby.

Chapter Six

Dear Editor,

In response to the most recent letter written to this newspaper by *Fired Up in Lovestruck*, I submit the following:

Three Reasons Why I Refuse to Accept Fired Up's Apology:

1. Fired Up in Lovestruck continued his ceaseless attack on my work in the second paragraph of the letter, effectively negating

any goodwill he'd managed to foster with his brief, two-sentence apology.

2. A proper apology should be directed at the person who was slighted, not that person's employer.

3. Listicles are a thing. Get used to it.

I could go on, but three seems like a nice place to stop—a perfectly thorough list, by any definition.

Sincerely,
Queen Bee

"So how was it?" Aunt Alice slid a bowl of oatmeal topped with a generous helping of cinnamon-baked apples in front of Madison, then turned her attention back to her knitting.

Beneath the table, Toby pawed at Madison's shins. She didn't bother pushing him away, nor did she take a bite of the breakfast her aunt had so lovingly prepared for her. She couldn't, even if she'd wanted to.

She'd never been so exhausted in her life. She was tired to the bone. It was a miracle she'd even managed to make her way home from Jack's house.

"Coffee." She pushed herself to her feet and shuffled toward the kitchen counter. "Now."

The clickety-clack of Alice's knitting needles came to a halt. "Oh, dear. It was that bad?"

"I just…" Madison shook her head. Words failed her, and that *never* happened. She made her living off words! "Those twins are adorable, but wow. Why didn't anyone ever tell me how much *work* babies are? I can't even hold them properly, unless they're asleep. How do actual parents do this?"

No wonder Jack Cole was so cranky all the time. He was completely outnumbered in his own home.

"Um, isn't that precisely what Fired Up in Lovestruck tried to tell you two weeks ago? Don't you remember? It was right after your column about which babies to follow on Instant Pot."

"Instagram," Madison said between gulps of coffee.

Looking back, maybe that column hadn't been her best. Entertaining, certainly. But helpful in any way when it came to actual parenting? Not so much.

No wonder Mr. Grant wanted her to get some hands-on experience with children. After the first half hour at Jack's house, she'd been ready to pack it in.

She couldn't go back there. Absolutely not.

"Are you sure it's Instagram? Instant Pot sounds more familiar." Aunt Alice frowned.

"I'm sure. You look at pictures on Instagram. I'm not entirely sure what an Instant Pot is for, but it involves cooking." That was her problem in a nutshell, wasn't it? She knew nothing about domestic life—not about cooking or cleaning or what kind of hair appliance might burn down a barn, and even less about babies.

She'd had to Google just about everything—how to heat up a bottle, how to change a diaper, what to do when they cried. Maybe it wouldn't have been so terrible if she hadn't been outnumbered. But there were *two* of them. She hadn't stood a chance. The only time she hadn't been on the verge of tears was when she'd fallen asleep in the massive swishy chair in the twins' bedroom, a baby in each arm.

That chair was a godsend. Whoever had invented it should be awarded a Nobel Peace Prize…or three.

"Anyway, I can't believe you're quoting Fired Up in Lovestruck. I'm more furious than ever at that creep." She refilled her mug to the brim.

At this rate it was going to take half a pot to make it through breakfast and get to the office on time. She needed a shower, too. Her hair was dotted with cereal, and she didn't even want to identify the mustard-colored stain on her blouse. Coco Chanel was probably rolling in her grave.

"Why?" Alice brushed past her to scoop Toby's breakfast out of the bag of premium dog food she kept in the pantry. Like everything else in Vermont, it was maple-flavored. "You proved your point about the applesauce. He apologized, didn't he?"

Madison rolled her eyes. "Please. That was hardly an apology."

In truth, Fired Up's lame attempt at saying he was sorry didn't have anything to do with her current indignation. She was angry at him because his letters were the reason she was working two jobs at the moment.

But mostly, she was furious because he'd been right about her all along.

She knew that now. One night caring for Jack Cole's little girls had taught her a thing or two. Mostly, it had confirmed the fear she'd managed to bury deep inside all her adult life—she wasn't cut out to be a mother.

Tears welled in her eyes, and she blinked hard. She'd been on the fast track since she'd graduated from Columbia, determined to make a name for herself in Manhattan. She'd always loved fashion and for a while, she'd thought about going to Parsons School of Design. Her dad had been the one to steer her toward fashion journalism instead, suggesting it might the safer choice. The secure choice.

She'd thought she'd simply been emulating her father. He'd been a powerhouse, a corporate legend. Madison had been less than a year old when her mom died, so she had no idea what kind of man Edward Jules had been before fate had cast him into the role of single dad. The father she'd grown up with had been one who'd taught her to work for a life built on a solid foundation. Taking the safe and logical route meant never having the rug swept out from under you. It meant *security*. It meant control—inasmuch as life could be controlled.

Madison adored her dad, so of course she'd chosen to follow in his footsteps. She'd found a way to pursue her dreams of a job in fashion the smart way, the practical way. She was her father's daughter, through and through. But despite all her efforts to safeguard her life, she'd been laid off. Since her dad's fatal heart attack five years ago, her career had been her entire life. And she'd lost that life in the blink of an eye, in the same sort of heartbreaking efficiency with which she'd lost her father.

Madison had been so busy trying to get her life back that she hadn't stopped to think about everything she'd given up for her success.

Until now.

She knew her dad's intentions had been good. He'd only been trying to protect his little girl from further pain. Further loss. But maybe there was more to life than simply feeling safe and secure. After all, a life without loss was a life without love.

So yeah. In a moment of weakness, she'd seen those two sweet babies and they'd reminded her so much of herself at their age that she'd actually *wanted* the nanny job. She'd wanted to dote on Ella and Emma and perhaps find a part of herself that had been lost all those years ago.

What a fool she'd been. There wasn't a maternal bone in her body. No wonder her parenting column was such a disaster that a critic had made it his own personal mission to make her life miserable. Fired Up in Lovestruck knew the truth.

"I'm going to quit," she said quietly.

Aunt Alice's hand fluttered to her chest. "Your column?"

"No, of course not. The nanny job. It's—" Madison swallowed around the lump in her throat "—it's just not for me. I don't have time. I don't know what I was thinking."

"I thought it was only two or three times a week? Just the nights that Sarah's son has off from the fire station."

"It is." Madison shrugged, feigning nonchalance. "But look at me. I'm a mess. I've had maybe three hours of sleep and I have to work today. At my *real* career."

"Okay, then. Whatever you think is best, dear," her aunt said, supportive as always.

But her heart wasn't in it. Madison could hear the slight hint of disappointment in her tone, and it was like an arrow to her heart.

Join the club, she wanted to say. No one was more disappointed in Madison than she was in herself.

Maybe she should tell her aunt about the baby powder explosion she'd created when she'd dropped the container and it had bounced from the end table to the sofa to the floor. Or perhaps she should share the fact that it had taken her four tries to get the rice cereal right and probably glued a bowl permanently to the inside of the microwave in the process. Even the clothes had been tough to figure out. Did infant pajamas really need 10,000 snaps?

As for the diaper situation…it was beyond description.

As humiliating as those mistakes had been, nothing had been as mortifying as waking up just before dawn, stumbling into the den and realizing that at some point during the night, Jack had gotten up and cleaned every inch of the mess she'd made. The sight of the pristine kitchen had nearly made her weep from shame. He was going to fire her. *Obviously.* Any sane person would.

Her only saving grace had been the fact that Sarah showed up promptly at six in the morning, before Jack had even emerged from his bedroom. By some miracle, Emma and Ella had also been asleep in their cribs. Sarah couldn't stop gushing about what a wonderful job she'd done, and Madison just couldn't take it. She'd slunk away before Jack even made an appearance.

And now here she stood in her aunt's kitchen, too

ashamed to admit the truth: she was a horrendous night nanny, and Jack's baby girls deserved better. They deserved the world.

Madison took a bite of her oatmeal. It was delicious, but for some silly reason, the homey flavors of nutmeg, cinnamon and apples made her want to cry all over again.

She looked up, and her aunt cast her a questioning glance.

Are you sure you want to quit?

The question was written all over the older woman's face. Even Toby was looking at her with wide, penetrating eyes.

"I just can't do it," Madison said, and it might have been the most honest thing she'd uttered all morning.

It was a good thing Jack had finally gotten some sleep, because the morning awaiting him at the fire station was the busiest he'd had in quite some time.

First up was a motor vehicle collision on the highway on the outskirts of town. Engine Co. 24 was the first to arrive on the scene, which involved multiple injuries. Luckily, everyone was fairly easily patched up. One of the drivers and a few passengers required transport to the big hospital up in Burlington, but none of the injuries appeared to be life-threatening.

Just minutes after the crew returned to the station, they got another call for a small grass fire at the local junior high, which turned out to be the result of some kids messing around with firecrackers behind the gym. Jack and Wade had the fire out within minutes, but they'd spent nearly an hour educating the culprits as to the dangers of fireworks. It was the sort of call that Jack used to love best—a chance to personally get involved with the residents of Lovestruck, beyond issuing permits or putting out fires.

In recent months he'd lost his passion for interacting with members of the community. Sometimes, as much as he hated to admit it, dealing with the good citizens of Lovestruck made Jack feel like the list of people who wanted or needed something from him was longer than he could manage.

Today he felt different. Some of his spark was back. He didn't want to think too hard on why he felt like the old Jack Cole, nor did he want to get into another big discussion about his personal life with his coworkers over breakfast. He just wanted to enjoy it, which was why he was the first to volunteer for the third call of the day. It was the call that every member of Engine Co. 24 dreaded most— Ethel Monroe's cat, Fancy, was stuck at the top of her old sugar maple tree again.

"No way." Brody didn't even bother glancing up from the report he was working on for the traffic accident call. "I did it last time, and I've still got the scratches to prove it."

"I'm pulling rank. That cat is a demon. Besides, I'm allergic," Cap said as he hung up the phone with dispatch.

"Can't we just tell Ethel to wait it out? Ask her if she's ever seen a cat skeleton in a tree before. I guarantee the answer is no." Brody shook his head. "Fancy will eventually come down on her own. Firefighters in Birmingham would never respond to a cat-in-a-tree call."

"I'll do it." Jack closed his laptop on the high school grass fire report, nearly complete.

"Wait. What?" Brody finally looked up. "You're *volunteering* to rescue that nightmare?"

"You heard me." Jack stood. "But Wade's got to come along and handle the ladder while I climb up there."

"I'm in." Wade shrugged. "So long as I don't have to go anywhere near the cat. That thing is a monster and, like Brody, I'm fundamentally opposed to perpetuating the myth that we save kittens from trees."

It wasn't a myth, though. Not in Lovestruck, anyway.

Firefighters didn't actually rescue cats from trees in big cities, but in rural Vermont, anything went. Last year alone, Engine 24 had responded to four calls for cat rescues, and three of those calls had involved Fancy. One of these days Ethel Monroe's cranky Persian was going to remember that she was terrified of heights, but today was not that day.

"Come on," Jack said, grabbing his turnout gear. He didn't want to get caught without it if something happened to catch on fire before they got back to the station. Also, Brody wasn't exaggerating. Jack had seen the scratches on his arms and they weren't pretty.

A couple hours later Fancy was safely back inside Miss Ethel's cottage. Despite his turnout gear, Jack suffered a few minor scratches—mostly on his face—and returned to the firehouse dressed in cargo pants, his LFD T-shirt and a sizable adhesive bandage on his left cheek. Wade had done the patching up for him, so of course the bandage wasn't a regular, flesh-colored one, but was instead decorated with colorful cartoon Dalmatians.

All in a day's work. Somehow Jack's good humor remained mostly intact. But when he climbed down from the ladder truck and saw Madison Jules sitting primly on the teak park bench outside the firehouse, his spirits soared foolishly higher.

Get ahold of yourself.

He cleared his throat and pretended nothing was out of the ordinary as he walked up the long drive toward the station. Beside him, Wade droned on about something that Jack completely ignored. He tried his best to keep his gaze straight ahead, but it was practically impossible. As usual, Madison looked woefully out of place for Lovestruck. She wore bright red stilettos and a floaty dress—sleeveless, white with black polka dots and a soft bow tied at her throat. It occurred to him that her fancy ensemble almost matched his cartoon bandage, and he bit back a smile. The way she always stuck out like a sore thumb was beginning to grow on him.

What was wrong with him?

Surely, she wasn't there to see him. She'd probably stopped by on some type of official business. Maybe she needed someone to inspect a new flat iron or blow-dryer.

"Wait a minute." Wade's steps slowed as he squinted at Madison sitting in the shade of the American flag flapping in the light summer breeze. "Isn't that…?"

Before Jack could respond, Madison's eyes lit up with recognition, and she stood to give him a tentative wave. Jack waved back as Wade's eyes went wide.

"Is she here to see *you*?" Wade said under his breath as they drew closer. "Well done, man."

"Shut. Up." Jack shot him a death glare. "It's not what you think."

Wade's only response was a gigantic smirk, which Jack could do nothing about because they'd just about reached the park bench where Madison stood waiting for him.

"Hi." Her gaze moved over his face, and her expression went from worried to amused and back again. "I feel like I should ask if you're hurt, but I can't get past the irony of your Dalmatian Band-Aid."

"The bandage was my idea." Wade raised his hand. "Glad you like it."

"I'm fine," Jack said, but no one seemed to be listening.

"He's just a little scratched up from rescuing a kitten in a tree," Wade interjected, oh so helpfully.

Madison laughed. "Seriously? That's a real thing that you do?"

"He does." Wade nodded. "He also rescues other cute animals. Last week it was a pair of ducklings stuck in a storm drain."

For the love of God, would he *stop talking* already?

Jack raked a hand through his hair, tugging hard at the ends. Time to set the record straight before Wade started planning their wedding. "Wade, this is Madison Jules. She's my…"

Night nanny.

The words were right there on the tip of his tongue, but Madison interrupted before he could get them out.

"Um, actually I need to talk to you about the whole nanny thing," she said, smile faltering.

And that was all it took for something in Jack's gut to harden into stone.

"Well." Wade shifted awkwardly from one foot to the other. "I'll let you two chat. It was nice to see you again, Madison."

"Nice to see you, too." She grinned, but it didn't reach her eyes the way it always seemed to do when she was busy arguing with Jack.

Despite the warning bells currently going off in his head, a proprietary surge of awareness flowed through his veins. Good grief, he was a mess.

"So," he said once Wade was out of earshot. "What can I help you with, Madison?"

She took a deep breath, and then her face crumpled. "Stop it, would you?"

He blinked. What had he done now? "Stop what?"

"Stop being so nice and…and—" she glared at his bandage "—*heroic*," she spat, as if it was a dirty word.

Jack wanted to laugh, but he didn't dare. "I'll do my best."

"Honestly. Could you please just go ahead and do it?" She wrapped her arms around herself as if it took every ounce of her strength to hold herself together, and Jack was reminded of the lecture Wade had given him on the rig after the first time he'd seen her.

Don't you think she seemed a little vulnerable?

He'd scoffed at the idea back then, but suddenly it didn't seem so far off base.

"Madison." He had to bite his tongue to keep himself from tacking an endearment onto her name. *Honey. Sweetheart. Darlin'*. Why did he keep forgetting she was his *employee*? "I'm not sure what all this is about."

Over her shoulder, Jack spotted Wade, Cap and Brody watching them through the upstairs kitchen window, and he wished they were having this conversation someplace else other than the front steps of the firehouse. *Any*place else.

He lowered himself onto the bench, which wasn't entirely out of view, but better.

Then he patted the empty space next to him. "Talk to me. Please?"

She sat down gingerly beside him, all womanly softness and polka dot chiffon. God, she smelled fantastic—like daisies and sunlight, with just a telltale hint of baby powder.

"I'm fired," she said succinctly. "There. If you won't say it, I will."

He reached for her hand with his, then caught himself and rested his empty palm in his lap instead. "You're not fired."

"Oh, please. I *so* am. And I definitely deserve it. I'm sorry to barge in at your workplace like this, but I thought it would be best to get this over with so you'd have time to find someone else to take care of the girls." She gave him a decisive nod. "Someone better."

He looked at her long and hard. He didn't want someone better. He wanted *her*. "Still not firing you. Sorry."

Her gaze narrowed. "Fine. Then I quit."

"Resignation not accepted." He stood and planted his hands on his hips. "Now that we've got that all settled, I should probably get back to work. There's probably a baby animal in need of saving somewhere."

She flew to her feet just as he started to walk away. "Wait!"

He arched a brow. "Is there something else?"

She studied him for a quiet moment, and something unspoken passed between them—something beyond banter and bravado—something *real*. And a strange sort of joy bubbled up inside Jack as he got his first glimpse of what it might feel like to be on Madison's good side.

"Toby is a Chinese crested," she blurted without preamble.

Jack was lost again. Keeping up with this woman was a full-time job. "A what?"

"A Chinese crested. It's a type of dog." She pulled a face. "A hairless one. He's got an impressive collection of hand-knit sweaters, though."

So Toby the three-year-old who worshipped her

was, in fact, a dog. That explained the baby powder. And the diapers. And the rest of the mess she'd made.

"I would expect nothing less than a stellar wardrobe for the canine in your life," he deadpanned.

"He's not technically *mine*. He belongs to my aunt. I'm staying with them for a while."

A while. Jack tensed, and he wasn't entirely sure why.

He shrugged. "You're still not fired."

"But I lied," she countered.

"We all lie from time to time," he said, thinking of his letters to the *Lovestruck Bee*. He'd been actively lying about his own identity to a stranger in the newspaper *every single day*. For weeks. "We'll see you Friday night, Madison. Ella and Emma are looking forward to it."

So was he, but Jack didn't say so.

We all lie from time to time.

A lie by omission was a lie, all the same.

Chapter Seven

Dear Editor,

With all due respect, if listicles *are indeed a thing, as Queen Bee insists, I shudder to think what will come of children's storybooks.*

Sincerely,
Fired Up in Lovestruck

Dear Editor,

I can't help but wonder how Fired Up in Lovestruck feels about Goldilocks and the Three Bears?

The Three Little Pigs?
One Fish, Two Fish, Red Fish, Blue Fish?
The Three Billy Goats Gruff?

I could go on, but I have a column to write.
My point—even kids love lists. How does
Fired Up think they learn to count?

Sincerely,
Queen Bee

Dear Queen Bee,

Touché. You got me.

Sincerely,
Fired Up in Lovestruck

The following Saturday morning Madison couldn't help feeling just a tiny bit triumphant as she walked to the library for her volunteer shift at story hour.

The night before she'd somehow managed to survive another shift at Jack's house with his adorable twins. They slept even less than they had during her first attempt at night nannying, but at least she knew how to properly diaper and feed them. They just never seemed to want to do those things at the same time, which was most inconvenient. While Ella slept, Madison took care of Emma. Then once Emma drifted off, Ella would invariably wake up and the cycle would start all over again.

She finally got them both down for the night around three in the morning, thanks to the glider rocker and an early copy of the September issue of *Vogue.* She read the pages aloud to them for almost an hour. Maybe it was only her imagination, but they seemed to love it. Once she had the babies tucked back into their cribs, Madison cleaned up a little bit. She even did a load of Jack's laundry—her way of saying thanks for not being fired.

Had she buried her face into his LFD T-shirt, just to get a whiff of his manly, kitten-saving scent? Yes. Yes, she had. She wasn't proud of that little moment of weakness, but she couldn't quite help it. The soft cotton material had felt so good against her cheek, and the woodsy aroma of cypress smoke and fresh summer air was somehow comforting and enticing, all at once.

Maybe it was time to admit that Jack Cole wasn't entirely terrible. In a purely platonic way, of course.

Because platonic friends go around sniffing each others' laundry all the time.

Madison rolled her eyes at herself as she walked up the front steps of the Lovestruck Public Library to the sounds of church bells marking the hour as they always did, seven days a week. She'd decided to chalk the embarrassing laundry incident up to sleep deprivation. It wouldn't be repeated, nor would she linger every so often outside Jack's closed bedroom door and listen to the rhythmic sound of his breathing, wondering if he ever dreamed about her.

He clearly didn't.

There was just something so unexpectedly intimate about being in a man's home while he slept. A house says a lot about a person, and Madison loved the bookshelves in Jack's living room, filled with cracked spines and beloved classics like *Where the Red Fern Grows* and *Call of the Wild*. She loved the fact that there were even a few books of poetry tucked in between the novels and that Jack did the *Lovestruck Bee*'s Sunday crossword puzzle. She knew more about him than she should have; that was all. She wasn't developing actual *feelings* for him. That would just be crazy.

He'd been so nice to her when she'd tried to quit the nanny job, though. Far nicer than she'd deserved, since she'd definitely overstated her experience with babies in order to snag the position. And when he'd sat down beside her on the park bench outside the fire station a few days ago, she could have sworn he'd almost reached for her hand. Just the thought of it had caused her palm to go all tingly.

Who *was* she, and what had she done with the real Madison Jules?

She was supposed to be concentrating on getting out of Lovestruck and back to Manhattan, where babysitting and holding hands with firemen on quaint park benches were nowhere on her radar. Now wasn't the time to succumb to the charms of small-town Vermont or its heroic inhabitants. Her column was gaining serious ground, and at long last, her meanie pen pal had caved and admitted she'd been right about something. Oh, glorious day.

Madison took a deep breath as she walked into the hushed interior of the library and reached into the pocket of the oversize knit sweater Alice had insisted she start wearing to her night nanny shifts. She'd tucked the latest letter from Fired Up in Lovestruck inside so she could take it out and reread it when she needed an extra shot of confidence.

The only thing that would have made his short and sweet missive any better was if Mr. Grant would have printed it in the newspaper. On the front page, preferably. In sixty-point font.

Mr. Grant couldn't print it at all, though, because unlike his other letters, this one hadn't been addressed to the editor. It had been written to Madison personally. She wasn't sure what to make of that significant detail. On one hand, it was possible that Fired Up in Lovestruck was simply trying to avoid publicly admitting her column wasn't complete and total garbage.

But at the same time, she sort of liked the intimacy of a letter addressed just to her. At least he seemed to view her as a real living, breathing person now instead of just a faceless reporter churning out a "whimsical dribble of words" on the regular.

In any case, she decided to hold on to the letter so she could refer back to it the next time she was feeling terrible about the sad state of her journalism career. Her phone hadn't exactly been ringing off the hook with interview requests at fashion magazines, so she could certainly use a pep talk every now and then—even a pep talk that consisted of a mere four words.

Touché. You got me.

"Oh, hi!" A woman with piles of blond hair twisted into a ballerina bun peered at Madison over the tall stack of books in her arms. "You must be Madison. Alice told us you'd be coming by today to read to the children. I'm Honey, the head librarian."

"Hello. It's nice to meet you." On instinct, Madison stuck out her hand.

Honey juggled her books to one arm and attempted an awkward shake. "Sorry, I'm in the middle of shelving. We've got about fifteen minutes until story hour, but kids are already starting to arrive and get settled."

Madison glanced toward the children's section of the library, where half a dozen toddlers and elementary school—aged kids were sitting cross-legged around a white rocking chair.

"Why don't you pick out a few books to read? The picture books are all shelved along the far wall. There are plenty, so I'm sure you can find something fun."

"Oh, sure." Madison nodded as if she had any clue what kind of book might be appropriate for the children of Lovestruck.

She'd sort of assumed that the librarian would select the books, but Honey was already bustling toward the general fiction shelves, pausing along the way to help an older patron who seemed to be having trouble using one of the community computers.

Okay, then.

She could do this. If she could handle eight straight hours with twin six-month-olds, she could certainly handle story time at the library. And once it was over, she'd head straight back to Aunt Alice's and take the mother of all naps. Her part-time night nanny gig was proving to be more exhausting than the cocktail circuit on the Upper East Side.

She headed straight for the shelf labeled with a little castle insignia that read Fables & Fairy Tales. Right off, she found *The Three Little Pigs*, *Goldilocks and the Three Bears* and *Three Billy Goats Gruff*, all stories she'd mentioned in her recent retort to Fired Up in Lovestruck. They'd worked for her column, so she supposed they'd work for story time, too. The Dr. Seuss collection was situated nearby, where Madison spotted *One Fish, Two Fish, Red Fish, Blue Fish* on the bottom shelf.

Why not?

She bent to grab it on her way to the story circle, but the moment she returned to an upright position, she plowed straight into a wall of muscle—and that wall just happened to be wearing a helmet and a good deal of fire-retardant clothing.

"J-Jack," she managed to sputter as she crashed facefirst into his chest. There was that smoky smell again, this time mixed with the gentle aroma of fresh, clean soap.

He reached for her shoulders, holding her steady as the books in her arms slid to the floor in a pile of rhyming verse and whimsical illustrations. "Whoa, there. Sorry, I didn't mean to frighten you."

"You didn't." She shook her head hard enough for a long curl to fall in front of one of her eyes. She still longed for her flat iron on a daily basis. "I mean, I'm not scared."

Liar, liar, pants on fire.

Everything about Jack frightened her—from the way the low timbre of his voice caused heat to swarm low in her belly to the protective warmth of his big hands and everything in between. Oh, no. She really was developing feelings for him, wasn't she? Her pants might actually be on fire.

A hysterical little laugh bubbled up her throat. *Oh, my God. Get a grip, it's only a harmless crush.*

"You sure you're okay?" Jack studied her.

"Just peachy."

He released his grip on her, and for a moment every cell in her body seemed to weep at the loss of contact. Then he reached to brush the hair from her eyes and tuck it tenderly behind her ear, and a riot of goose bumps broke out over her neck and all the way down her arm.

"Ahem." She coughed to keep herself from purring like a kitten. "Ahem. What are you doing here… in all of your, um, regalia?"

"Regalia?" He laughed, and it occurred to Madison that Jack didn't do so nearly often enough. "It's just turnout gear. Hardly regal."

Agree to disagree.

He gestured toward the library's circulation desk, where Honey was chatting with another uniformed firefighter. "I'm here with Wade. We're doing the biannual inspection of the library's fire extinguishers. And you? Are you here picking up a little light reading?"

He smiled, then bent to gather the storybooks, still scattered at their feet.

Madison knelt beside him and righted the overturned copy of *The Three Little Pigs*. "Actually, I'm volunteering. I'm reading at the children's story hour. It starts in just a few minutes, so I was getting a few books together."

Jack's gaze locked on to the book in her hands, and his smile faded ever so slightly. "Volunteering. That's great."

"My aunt Alice suggested it," Madison said.

Jack nodded absently as he gathered himself back to his full height and took a closer look at the books he'd picked up from the floor. A few more children entered the library and skipped toward the story circle while their parents ambled behind them, clutching coffee cups from the Lovestruck Bean.

Madison would have killed for a maple latte right then. Who knew you could bring food and beverages into the library? Once again, things in Vermont were proving to be breezy and relaxed…

With the notable exception of the air swirling between her and Jack. He'd gone stony-faced all of a sudden. Any and all traces of earlier camaraderie seemed to vanish so quickly that Madison wondered if the flirty vibe she'd picked up on had only been the product of wishful thinking.

"Um, I should probably head on over there," she said, tipping her head in the direction of the children, who'd begun crawling all over each other in anticipation.

He looked up finally, brow furrowed, and handed the picture books back to her. "Interesting selection. Any reason why you chose those particular books?"

"Sort of." Madison shrugged. She kept forgetting that the few people she knew in Lovestruck didn't realize she wrote for the newspaper. Ah, the joys of being forced to write under a cutesy pseudonym. It wasn't exactly a state secret, though. She should probably tell him. "Actually, I..."

"Madison!" Honey waved at her from the story circle. "We're ready for you!"

Madison waved back and cast one last look at Jack. Was it her imagination, or did he look oddly pale? "Sorry. Duty calls."

"Of course," he said woodenly. "Go."

She lingered for a moment, tempted to stay so she could try and figure out why he was acting so strangely. Silly, really. There were children waiting for her, and since when had Jack and his moody streak become her problem?

"Right. See you later," she said, squaring her shoulders as she walked away.

She didn't have any intention of making a life here, with or without a brooding fireman and his darling twin babies. She didn't even *like* Vermont. Jack Cole wasn't hers, and he never would be. Those were the simple facts.

Madison just wasn't sure when or why they'd become so difficult to remember.

"Locking pin intact?" Wade said, glancing down at the inspection checklist on the screen of the tablet in his hand.

The question barely registered in Jack's consciousness as he stood listening to Madison read aloud from the rocking chair on the other side of the room. She had such a lovely voice—soft and soothing. Or that was how it had seemed the night before as he lay in bed listening to her read to the girls through the wall. Who knew articles about the latest runway shows and the eternal popularity of animal prints could be so relaxing?

But that was the whole point of reading aloud to infants, wasn't it? Reading to babies was a bonding experience. Jack knew this. The subject matter wasn't as important as tone of voice, facial expressions and gentle touch—unless the subject matter happened to be the exact four books that Queen Bee had mentioned in her most recent letter to the editor.

"Yo," Wade whisper-screamed at him. They were, after all, in a library. "Are we here to inspect the fire extinguishers or to spy on your night nanny?"

"The locking pin is intact, the tamper seal is unbroken and there are no signs of obvious damage, so you can check those things off your list." Jack lifted the device from the wall so he could estimate its weight and ensure it was still full. "And I'm not spying. I had no idea she'd be here."

"I'm telling you, it's fate." Wade tapped away on the tablet. "The way you two keep bumping into each other might just mean something."

"I'm beginning to think fate might have a twisted sense of humor," Jack said, securing the fire extinguisher back into place and scrawling his initials and the date on its tag.

"Uh-oh. I know that tragic tone in your voice. And just when you seemed to be somewhat happy for a change." Wade frowned. "What happened?"

Jack brushed past him, headed toward the next fire extinguisher on their list—the one behind the circulation desk. "Nothing happened."

Nothing at all.

He *wished* something had. There. He'd admitted it, even if only to himself. He couldn't stop thinking about Madison.

"And nothing's going to," he added, not entirely sure whether that disclaimer was for his own benefit or Wade's.

"Why not? Is it the nanny thing? Because no one cares." Wade shrugged. "You're hot for Mary Poppins. Admit it."

Jack rolled his eyes. "She's hardly Mary Poppins."

"Are you seeing what I'm seeing?" Wade's gaze

cut toward Madison, reading the part of Baby Bear from *Goldilocks and the Three Bears* in a goofy, high-pitched voice that made the children sitting at her feet collapse into giggles. "Those kids are spellbound."

Join the club.

Jack turned his back on the adorable scene and focused intently on the red fire extinguisher fixed to the wall, but he couldn't bring himself to continue the inspection. "I think she might be Queen Bee."

"Who?"

There was a beat of confused silence until Wade gasped so loud he started coughing. Nearly every head in the library swiveled in their direction. Jack gave Wade a firm slap on the back.

"Would you *please* be quiet," he muttered.

"I'm fine!" Wade waved to the library patrons, and Madison continued reading. Then he stared hard at Jack and whispered, "I lied. I'm *not* fine. Are you telling me that Madison is the reporter from the newspaper who you've been publicly shaming for *weeks*?"

When put that way, his behavior sounded really bad.

Jack groaned. Who was he kidding? It *was* bad, no matter how he sliced it. "Yes? Maybe? I'm not sure, but I've got a really bad feeling it might be true."

"Why?"

"The books she's reading to the kids right now are the same ones Queen Bee wrote about recently in the paper." He ground his teeth and did his best to ignore Madison's bell-like voice. *Somebody has been sitting in my chair!*

The children echoed her. *Somebody has been sitting in my chair!*

Jack closed his eyes. *Somebody* had been writing asinine letters to the newspaper, and now he was going to have to pay the price.

"Wait, that sounds like Goldilocks," Wade said. He rolled his eyes. "That's one of the most popular kids' books ever. It could just be coincidence."

"What about the other three? The Dr. Seuss book, plus the pigs and the billy goats."

"All classics. I think you're jumping to conclusions." Wade shot him an encouraging glance, but it wasn't altogether convincing.

"I'm not sure mathematical odds would support that theory." Jack turned his attention back to the fire extinguisher, lest Madison glance his way.

She couldn't possibly be Queen Bee, could she? Why would someone with a full-time job at the *Lovestruck Bee* want to take on the added responsibilities of caring for twin six-month-olds at night? Granted, the night nanny job was only part-time. *Very* part-time, now that he thought about it. She only worked on nights he was off duty from the station and since his schedule was three nights on, one night off, it boiled down to just a couple nights per week. Definitely not enough of a salary to live on.

But she lived with her aunt, so maybe she didn't need to work full-time in order to survive?

He felt like banging his head against the hard metal of the fire extinguisher all of a sudden. How much did he actually know about Madison Jules?

"Nope." Wade shook his head and acted like he was scribbling something onto his checklist. "They can't be the same person. Didn't you say your mom met Madison at a knitting class? And look, now she's volunteering at story circle. Your reporter wouldn't be caught dead doing either of those things."

True… Possibly.

The whole reason he'd started complaining about her column was its lack of practical information for parents. Whoever had been writing it didn't seem to have any actual real-life experience with children. Queen Bee couldn't possibly be the sort of person who'd knit baby booties or read to kids in her spare time.

But she'd definitely be the type who wouldn't know how to change a diaper. Or properly mix baby cereal. Or heat up a bottle.

"She's not *my* reporter. Don't say that," Jack said, even as a terrible dread gathered in the pit of his stomach. "We just write letters to each other. *Hostile* letters. Queen Bee is a complete and total stranger."

Wade nodded.

Subject dropped, they got back to work as Madison kept turning the pages of her storybook. Jack couldn't help but follow along as he went through the motions of the inspection, but the timeless words she read aloud only reminded him of an ache that was becoming harder and harder to deny.

Somebody has been sleeping in my bed.

He could picture her there—her wild hair fanned over his pillow, her warm brown eyes looking up at him as he touched his lips to hers. He wanted her. He'd wanted her since the moment she'd reached over and plucked the apple out of his grocery cart like it was forbidden fruit. He'd nearly kissed her right then and there.

His throat went dry as he did his best to swallow the memory deep down, along with the ridiculous fantasy of Madison in his bed. It was never going to happen.

Especially if Queen Bee wasn't such a stranger, after all.

Chapter Eight

Dear Editor,

Have you stopped printing the letters from Fired Up in Lovestruck? It's been days since the last one appeared in the paper. I think I speak for the entire town when I say that we miss the banter between him and Queen Bee.

Sincerely,
Bored in Lovestruck

Dear Editor,

I just flipped through the entire newspaper and

couldn't find a single letter from Fired Up in Lovestruck or Queen Bee. Can I get a refund?
Sincerely,
Ripped Off in Lovestruck

Dear Editor,

Bring back Fired Up in Lovestruck!

Sincerely,
The Residents of Lovestruck Senior Center

Tuesday morning, after a blissful few days of silence from her nemesis, Madison was once again in the hot seat in Mr. Grant's office.

"Great. Now we've managed to anger the entire senior community of Lovestruck." Her boss wadded up his latest copy of the *Bee*'s front page and threw it at his computer monitor. It bounced back toward him, narrowly missing his face.

Madison winced. "Maybe it's not so bad. People are still talking about the column. That's good, right?"

"It's not good," Mr. Grant said flatly. "Not good at all. Subscriptions are down. Yesterday we had almost a dozen cancellations. Can you guess why?"

Madison shook her head. "Honestly, sir. I'd rather not."

Good grief, how was this happening? She'd lived in this town less than a month, and somehow she'd become responsible for the impending failure of the local paper.

Although, it wasn't actually her fault at all. It was *his*. Fired Up in Lovestruck had created this terrible mess, and just when Madison had figured out a way to work it to her advantage, he'd pulled a disappearing act.

At first, his silence had been a welcome relief. The short letter he'd addressed to her personally was still tucked into the pocket of her sweater, which she'd taken to wearing pretty much all the time. She couldn't help it. It was cozy and comfortable, and recently, it had begun to smell like Ella and Emma, fresh from a bath. Her former coworkers at *Vogue* would have probably died if they'd seen her pulling it on over her trendy Kate Spade jumpsuits and polka dot dresses, but there was zero chance of that happening since Madison was still stuck in Vermont.

So yeah, she needed a security blanket and the hand-knit sweater fit the bill. She didn't want to think too hard about why its baby powder and gentle lavender bubble bath scent made her want to close her eyes and breathe deep, because that was just…odd. She was a fashion journalist, not a parenting reporter. And definitely not an actual nanny.

The letter in her pocket proved that she was a professional—at least that had been her takeaway when she'd first read it. Her luck was turning around. Any day now, she'd get the call to go back to her regular life. Sooner or later, a position in fashion would open up, and when it did, she'd be on the first plane back to Manhattan.

Meanwhile, though, she'd apparently managed to anger her boss and the greater population of Lovestruck through no fault of her own whatsoever.

Damn you, Fired Up in Lovestruck.

Whoever that know-it-all man was, he was wreaking havoc on her day-to-day existence.

"We have to do something." Mr. Grant massaged the back of his neck, giving Madison a clear view of the sweat-stained armpits of his dress shirt. Lovely. "*You* have to do something."

She really did. Gruffness aside, she liked Mr. Grant. He reminded her a bit of her father. She felt bad being responsible for the sorry state of his dry cleaning, much less his newspaper. But how was she supposed to lure Fired Up out of hiding?

There was only one surefire way.

She sighed. "I'm going to have to write something really ridiculous. You realize that, don't you?"

Mr. Grant smiled. "Yep."

"Something even worse than the 'Top Ten Infants to Follow on Instagram,'" she said.

It seemed like a century had passed since she'd

whipped up that silly article. Her recent columns had been *filled* with useful information, thanks to Jack Cole and his twins. Now she was going to have to take a giant, humiliating step backward.

"I'm sure you can come up with something far worse." Mr. Grant's smile grew wider. "I have faith in your ability to craft something truly terrible and frivolous."

Madison wasn't sure whether to feel flattered or insulted. *Damn you* again, *Fired Up in Lovestruck.* "Yes, sir."

"Get to it. I need it by the end of the day." Mr. Grant waved a hand toward the bullpen.

Oh, joy.

Maybe it was a good thing she wrote under a ridiculous pseudonym, after all.

Since his run-in at the library with Madison, Jack had spent every spare moment the past few days compiling two lists—one detailing all the potential evidence that she was the writer behind the Queen Bee moniker, and the other outlaying all evidence to the contrary. He'd managed to come up with a solid argument for both scenerios. On one hand, it seemed entirely possible that she'd read Queen Bee's letter to the editor, just like everyone else in Lovestruck, and had simply chosen the library books because they'd been recommended by an "expert." On the other, she dressed like a runway model. Her stilettos alone were enough to convince him that she'd been responsible for writing "The Four Cutest Toddler Shoes for Fall."

By the time her next scheduled night nanny shift rolled around on Tuesday evening, Jack was certain of only two things: first, he needed to learn more about the woman he'd hired to care for his children while he slept. Second, he needed to stop writing the letters. He needed to *really* stop—no more backsliding and certainly no more sending letters addressed to Queen Bee personally.

Done, he thought, swigging a cup of coffee as he glanced at the clock above the stove. Madison was due to arrive any minute, and he was as nervous as an awkward kid waiting to ask his crush to prom.

Pathetic.

He rolled his eyes at himself. There was no logical reason for his anxiety. His need to know more about Madison was purely professional.

His eyes rolled even harder. Okay, *mostly* professional. Either way, tonight would be a fact-finding mission. It was not as if he would have gotten much sleep, listening to her quiet footsteps and gentle murmurs while he tried not to imagine running his fingertips along the perfect pink swell of her bottom lip.

Plus, he'd already stopped writing the letters. He'd quit completely cold turkey, even though for some insane reason, the idea that Madison might actually be Queen Bee gave him an almost undeniable urge to pick up a pen and paper.

He closed his eyes and let out a groan. God, he had it bad, didn't he? When Madison arrived, he should probably just let her in and make himself scarce like he always did, lest he act on his feelings—which would be absolutely crazy since he wasn't entirely sure *who* he had feelings for. Madison was a mystery and trying to unravel her would be fraught with complications.

The baby monitor on the kitchen counter crackled to life, and he could hear one of the girls start to babble. They'd been doing that more and more lately, especially Emma. He knew it was probably too early to expect to hear a *dada*, but he still caught himself holding his breath every now and then, hoping for the sweetest brand of miracle.

He strode down the hall and lifted Emma gently from her crib, holding her delicate little form against his chest.

"You," he whispered into her downy blond hair. "You're the one. You and your sister."

No one else. They were the most important people in the world, and they'd already been let down in the most painful possible way. Natalie had walked away without a backward glance. She'd even signed away her parental rights, even though he'd never asked for that as part of their divorce settlement. One day his daughters would grow up and find out that their mother had literally written them off as if they'd never existed. He was all they had now, and he owed it to them to devote himself to them wholeheartedly. He didn't have room in his life for distractions.

Not even a distraction as lovely as Madison Jules…or Queen Bee…or whoever the heck she was.

The doorbell rang as he bounced Emma in the crook of his elbow and right on cue, Ella started crying. Jack scooped her up in his free arm, and the symbolism wasn't lost on him as he strode to the door. His hands were both literally and figuratively full—too full to even let Madison into his home.

Or his life.

Even so, his rebellious heart pounded hard at the sight of her silhouette through the door's frosted glass window. "Come in, it's open."

She pushed the door open and swept into the house like a cool summer breeze, all tumbling hair and smooth, sun-kissed shoulders. He did a double take when he realized she was wearing kitten heels for a change—strappy little sandals, paired with a gingham sundress that made her look like she was on her way to a picnic in the park rather than the shadowy halls of his home in the wee hours of the night.

He took a deep breath and tried not to think about

how perfectly she'd tuck against him with her head nestled right beneath his chin. "Hello."

"Oh." Her beautiful face split into a wide grin at the sight of the babies in his arms. "Look who's up!"

"Yeah, sorry about that." He tipped his head toward Emma. "This one was babbling away in her crib, and as you know…"

"Once one twin is awake, the other is sure to follow." She glanced from the babies to him, and when their gazes locked, her smile turned bashful around the edges. "See? I'm learning."

Words in Jack's own handwriting tumbled through his head. *It's puzzling to me why the author of the parenting column seems to care more about aesthetics than actual children.*

He was ashamed to admit he'd written those words—and more—about anyone, but especially the woman standing in front of him. If he was right and Madison really was Queen Bee, she could never find out. She'd hate him for sure. It would certainly mean the end of whatever strange and wonderful friendship had begun to form between them, and he wasn't ready to give that up. The thought of it made his insides twist into a tight knot of panic.

He swallowed hard. "As long as we're all up and awake, I figured I could help you get the girls fed and bathed?"

Madison dropped her sweater and giant designer

tote on the kitchen table and shot him a puzzled look. "Isn't that my job? You've got kittens and ducklings to save tomorrow. You're supposed to be sleeping."

He couldn't help but laugh at her description of his workday. *Thanks a lot, Wade.*

"I'm not that tired yet." Another lie. He'd been chugging so much maple coffee from the Bean that the blood in his veins had probably been replaced with a mixture of caffeine and pancake syrup. "I can help you get the twins down and still get a few good hours of sleep in."

"Okay, then." Her gaze strayed toward his mouth, and a pink flush washed over her porcelain features before she looked away. "Great."

"Great," he echoed.

It was almost like he'd forgotten how to talk to a woman all of a sudden. He'd definitely forgotten what it was like to have one standing in his kitchen, other than his mom. He'd forgotten how a woman's presence could make everything seem brighter and full of light. The tension between his shoulder blades eased for the first time all day, and somewhere deep down he knew there wasn't another woman alive who had this effect on him.

Only her. Only Madison.

They spent the next hour or so feeding the twins, weaving around the high chairs, the sink and the butcher-block island as if they were part of some intimate, domestic dance. And despite the very real reasons why he shouldn't even be entertaining any sort of relationship with Madison, he loved the way she'd started to fit right into his life with the girls. He could have never predicted it when he'd answered the call out at her aunt's farmhouse and she'd had no idea her hair straightener had nearly started an electrical fire. But maybe that was just one of the things that made her special—she surprised him in the best possible ways, and it had been a long time since surprises had been kind to Jack.

He cleaned up the kitchen while Madison got Emma and Ella ready for their baths, trying his hardest to get his head screwed on straight while he scrubbed strained peas and carrots off the walls, the floor and himself. Thus far, his fact-finding mission had been an abysmal failure. He hadn't managed to ask Madison a single personal question, but mealtimes with the twins were always crazy. Surely, he could sneak in some adult conversation while they watched Emma and Ella splash in their bath seats. Trying to second-guess her every word and deed to see if it fit his imaginary profile of Queen Bee was going to be the end of him.

Maybe he should just come out and ask if it was her.

He considered this possibility as he tucked the twins' matching high chairs into the breakfast nook and flipped off the kitchen light. It was certainly direct. He just wasn't sure how to handle things afterward. Did he admit he was Fired Up in Lovestruck or just stick to his letter-writing embargo and keep his mouth shut?

Neither, he hoped. *Because she's* not *Queen Bee.*

Ella and Emma were snug in their bath seats in the tub, facing each other and kicking at the shallow water when Jack reached the bathroom. He lingered in the doorway for a moment, taking in the sight of Madison kneeling beside the tub, piling bubbles on top of a giggling Ella's head. His breathing grew slower. Calmer.

Madison caught sight of him over her shoulder and bit her lip. "You've got baby food on your shirt."

"Story of my life," he said, lowering himself next to her beside the tub.

She laughed far louder than he'd have expected.

"Are peas and carrots really so funny?" he said, dipping a finger into the bathwater and depositing a lavender-scented bubble on the tip of Madison's nose.

"Hey!" She blew at the bubble and it went airborne, capturing the attention of Emma and Ella's big blue eyes as it drifted overhead. "For your information, I wasn't laughing at the stain on your shirt. Not exactly, anyway. I was just thinking that I never, ever could have imagined you as a dad until that day we met at the Bean and you had Ella and Emma strapped to your chest in those cute sling carriers."

"You mean the day you caught me hiding from you?"

"Ha! I knew it!" She scooped a generous handful of bubbles from the tub and mashed them into his face.

The twins giggled in unison. As long as Jack lived, he'd never grow tired of his daughters' laughter. It was his favorite sound.

He shook his head, and bubbles flew everywhere. "Fine. I admit it. I kind of panicked when I realized you were the one interviewing for the night nanny job. The only reason I'm owning up to it now is that I'm fully prepared to admit how wrong I was. You're great with the girls."

"Really?" She blinked, clearly stunned by the compliment. "You think so?"

"I do." The second the words left his mouth, Jack realized they were straight from a wedding ceremony.

Do you take this woman, to have and to hold?
I do.

He cleared his throat. "I mean, yes. Definitely. I thought so that very first night." He felt one corner of his mouth lift into a half grin. "Baby powder explosion aside, I could just tell you were the perfect person for the job."

"Wow. That…" She inhaled a shaky breath. "That

might just be the nicest thing anyone has ever said to me."

"Surely, that's not true." He hoped to hell it wasn't. There had to be people in her life who believed in her and told her so on a regular basis. Everyone deserved that kind of support, especially someone as lovely and earnest as Madison.

He searched her gaze, trying desperately to unravel the complicated truth of who exactly she was as a shimmer of unshed tears gathered in her eyes.

"Sorry." She waved a hand and pasted on a smile that seemed a little too wide. "Don't mind me and my silly emotions."

"Please don't apologize," he said, and his voice sounded strange all of a sudden, like something rusty that hadn't been used in a while. A long, long while. "You're entitled to your feelings. It's not silly."

The smile wobbled off her face and what was left in its place was an expression so raw, so vulnerable that Jack almost felt like he should avert his gaze. But he couldn't seem to take his eyes off her. A hush fell between them, and the only sounds that registered in Jack's consciousness were the splash-splash of the twins in their bath seats and the beat of his own heart, pounding as if it had just recognized a kindred spirit.

"That day at the coffee shop you mentioned you'd

grown up without a mom," he finally said. "Is that what the sudden tears are about?"

She nodded. "In a way, yes. She died when I was just a baby, so it was always just me and my dad until he died a few years ago. I loved him very much, but I'm beginning to realize how much my mother's death shaped the way he raised me."

"How so?"

"To be strong, independent and practical, which are all great attributes, but…"

"But strength alone doesn't leave much room for connection." Jack nodded. He understood exactly what she was trying to say. How could he not? It was the same sentiment his mom and the guys at the firehouse had been repeating to him over and over again for the past year.

He hadn't wanted to hear it, though. He wasn't ready. He had his daughters, and they were the only connection he needed.

Or so he'd thought until his night nanny smiled at him from behind a veil of tears, and the urge to kiss her became so overwhelming that he could hardly breathe.

"Exactly." Her gaze slid toward the babies in the tub and then back toward him. "I suppose I owe you a thank-you. I was beginning to think I'd make a terrible mother someday, but now…"

Her voice went all soft around the edges, and the

gratitude in her expression just about killed him. He knew right then and there he could never, ever ask if she was Queen Bee. The answer to that question just might have the power to break a heart. Maybe even two.

"There's more to being a mother than knowing how to change a diaper, Madison. Simply showing up is a hell of a good start." He wasn't sure which one of them leaned in first or if they'd simply been drawn to each other by some invisible force, but she was suddenly *right there*, just a whisper away, so close that he could see the bloom of her pulse in the dip between her collarbones. He could see the heat in her eyes, as precious and unexpected as liquid gold. Somewhere deep inside, he felt himself slowly begin to crack open, and it felt so damn good, like he could take his first full gulp of oxygen after holding his breath for months.

He cupped her cheek in one of his hands—the lightest of touches, but it sent shock waves of awareness coursing through him, warm like honey. "You'll make a wonderful mother. Trust me."

"I trust you," she whispered, and the last shred of Jack's resistance fell away.

His gaze dropped to her perfect pink mouth and he dipped his head toward hers, almost undone by the thought of tasting her. The scent of lavender swirled in the air, wrapping them in a dream, and somehow

Jack summoned the wherewithal to send her a questioning look, because as much as he wanted this, he needed to know she wanted it, too.

She nodded, lips parting, and every cell in his body seemed to cry with relief. But in the final moment of sweet surrender, just as their lips were about to touch, two simple syllables dragged him away from the moment and back to reality.

Dada.

Madison's eyes flew open, and she found a shell-shocked Jack staring back at her less than an inch away. Goodness, he was a beautiful man. At this close range, his bone structure alone was almost enough to make her weep.

"Did you hear that?" he blurted.

She nodded. "I certainly did."

Dada. She'd heard it as plain as day, just when she'd thought nothing on God's green earth could have stopped her from kissing Jack Cole.

But this was a good interruption—an almost miraculous one, as evidenced by Jack's whoop of joy.

"I can't believe it." He shook his head and whooped again, then bent over the edge of the tub peering back and forth between Ella and Emma.

"Dada," he said. "Dada, dada, dada."

The girls let out twin squeals. Ella reached for Jack's nose and captured it in her tiny fist, and he laughed a deep belly laugh that made Madison feel like crying for some strange reason.

He shot her a quick glance. "Which one of them was it? Do you know?"

"I'm not sure." Some nanny she was. She'd been too busy kissing dada to tell which twin had just spoken her first word.

Almost kissing, technically.

It was a crucial difference. They hadn't actually locked lips, and for the life of her, Madison wasn't sure whether to be disappointed or relieved.

Okay, that was patently false. Her heart swelled for Jack and his *dada* moment, but she couldn't shake the sense of something unfinished—a moment of pure magic that had slipped right through her fingers.

It was for the best, though. She'd let herself get carried away by the kind things Jack had said to her, and for a wild, unguarded moment, she'd imagined that he and his little girls belonged to her. As crazy as it seemed, she'd almost believed that destiny had brought them into her life. Could it be that all this time, she'd been chasing a byline, longing for bigger and better things, when what she'd really needed was right here in Lovestruck?

Impossible.

"Dada," Jack said again, and this time, Emma giggled and let out a long stream of baby talk.

"A-ga, a-gagagaga." Her tiny face lit up in the

sweetest smile Madison had ever seen. "Dada. Da-dadadada."

Beside Madison, Jack's breath hitched, and it was suddenly too much for her to take. She wanted to throw her arms around him and join in the celebration. She wanted to capture the moment, snap a picture and paste it into a baby book with pink satin trim. She wanted to tell Jack that he was the very best father these two precious girls could ever want.

She didn't do any of those things, obviously. She couldn't. It wouldn't have been right, because this was a family moment, and Madison wasn't family. She was only the reporter who'd faked her way into a part-time night nanny job to further her career. To top it all off, her boss now wanted her to purposefully write something over-the-top ridiculous to court her worst critic.

So while Jack tended to his daughters, she slipped quietly out of the bathroom to let them have their moment and did her best to remind herself who—and what—she really was.

Chapter Nine

Dear Editor,

Are my eyes deceiving me, or is the subject of Queen Bee's latest column really How to Be-dazzle a Diaper?

I didn't want to write this letter. I really didn't, but out of concern for the safety and well-being of the children in our community, I feel compelled to point out the obvious: be-dazzling a diaper is dangerous. The "charms, rhinestones and glitter" that Queen Bee seems to think will make a disposable diaper "more *aesthetically pleasing" are, in fact, choking hazards.*

Also, disposable diapers are made of synthetic materials that are completely inappropriate for use with a hot glue gun. Honestly, this latest attempt at journalism is so egregious that I'm officially calling on you, the editor, to print a retraction clearly pointing out the dangers involved with diaper bedazzling—which I'm pretty sure isn't an actual thing.

Sincerely,
Fired Up in Lovestruck

Dear Editor,

While I'm disappointed to read that Fired Up in Lovestruck didn't appreciate the whimsical nature of my most recent column, I can't say I'm surprised.

Perhaps Fired Up missed the following note, which was included in fine print at the end of "How to Bedazzle a Diaper"?

Note: Queen Bee recommends bedazzling a diaper for special occasion photo shoots only—birthdays, #babymilestones, #selfiesaturday and the like. Not appropriate for everyday wear or use without close supervision.

Might I suggest a name change for Fired Up? I think Uptight in Lovestruck is still available.

Sincerely,
Queen Bee
Editor's Note:

The Lovestruck Bee does not condone or endorse gluing or in any way affixing small decorative items to disposable diapers. Not even for #babymilestones Instagram posts.

Dear Editor,

Thank you for your recent statement on diaper bedazzling.
Now...
Who's going to tell Queen Bee that babies, by their very nature, are incapable of participating in #sefliesaturday?

Sincerely,
Fired Up in Lovestruck

Madison sat at her desk, sipping her maple latte and feeling as if she was wrapped in a heavy blanket of cinnamon, sugar and shame.

Her ludicrous column about diaper bedazzling had worked. Mission accomplished—Fired Up in Lovestruck had taken the bait, and Mr. Grant was practically walking around the office on air. She should be thrilled, probably. But she couldn't help feeling like the biggest hack in the universe.

Obviously, she didn't think infants should be crawling around with rhinestones glued to their backsides. Honestly, she'd meant the whole thing more as satire than an actual craft project, hence her disclosure at the end of the article. If any of her readers actually managed to hot glue something onto a Pamper without melting it, she figured they would snap a cute photo and then toss the thing straight into the nearest trash can.

Mr. Grant had printed her endnote in the tiniest font imaginable, though. In her original draft, she'd typed the footnote in bold. No wonder Fired Up had gotten himself more fired up than ever. She didn't blame him one bit.

How long was she supposed to keep this up? She wasn't sure she could keep intentionally writing nonsense. It felt wrong on multiple levels. She was proud of the more helpful columns she'd penned lately. After a recent story on bedtime rituals for babies, she'd even gotten a few nice letters from parents, which she'd tacked to the wall of her cubicle.

They'd made her almost as happy as a trip to the *Vogue* closet.

And now all that good writing had been shot down by a glue gun and a handful of glitter.

What would Jack think if he knew about this?

She stared forlornly into her coffee. Jack Cole had nothing whatsoever to do with her career, so she wasn't sure why she'd all of a sudden begun to worry about his opinion.

His opinion mattered, though. It mattered more than it should, which terrified Madison. She cared too much about what he thought. She cared too much about *him*, period.

They'd nearly kissed two nights ago, and she'd hardly been able to concentrate on anything else since then. Other than diaper bedazzling, of course. She was distracted beyond reason. Case in point: she didn't notice Mr. Grant had come out of his office carrying a bullhorn until his gruff roar boomed throughout the room like it was the voice of God.

"Gather round, hive. I have important information." He waved everyone toward the center of the room and stood with his arms crossed, waiting for the worker bees to obey.

Madison glanced around, wondering whether this was a normal occurrence or something out of the ordinary. She'd yet to set eyes—or ears—on the bullhorn during her tenure at the *Bee*. Frankly, it seemed like overkill. They were a small-town paper with less than twenty total employees.

"It's got to be good news," Nancy, the food columnist, whispered as she shot Madison a grin. "He usually only pulls that thing out at the holiday party when he's about to distribute the Christmas bonuses."

Intriguing.

Madison joined her colleagues in the middle of the bullpen, standing on the fringe of the group until Mr. Grant called her forward.

"Madison, get up here. We've got you to thank for this." He smoothed down his dreadful brown tie. It was so comically out of fashion that Madison was beginning to think it was cute. Endearing, in a way.

She'd clearly been away from Park Avenue too long.

"Yes, sir." She made her way through the small crowd to stand beside him, more curious than ever.

"As all of you know, Madison's column has been attracting a lot of attention lately, which has given the *Bee* some great exposure. Everyone in Lovestruck has been buzzing about Queen Bee and her archenemy, Fired Up." Mr. Grant waggled his bushy gray eyebrows, and titters of laughter went up from the crowd.

A trickle of unease snaked its way up Madison's spine. She wanted less of Fired Up in Lovestruck in her life, not more. In fact, she would have been thrilled if he just disappeared altogether. Oh, how she wished her boss felt the same way.

I never should have written that diaper story.

What could possibly be next? Toddler hair extensions? Botox for babies?

"I'm pleased to say that a lot more people are going to be buzzing about your column really soon, Madison—*millions* of people, believe it or not," her boss said. He spoke his next words into the bullhorn, so they echoed throughout the *Bee*'s quaint newsroom loud enough to peel the sunny yellow paint off the walls. "Because you're going to be on the *Good Morning Sunshine* show tomorrow morning!"

His announcement was met with stunned silence for a second, and then everyone burst into cheers and applause. It all just sounded like white noise in Madison's head as she tried to make sense of what Mr. Grant had just said. *Good Morning Sunshine* was a national television show, filmed in New York. It had *millions* of viewers. Watching it was a morning ritual for half the country. Surely she wasn't supposed to get on national television and talk about a troll who seemed to have some strange obsession with her little local column. Just the thought of doing so made her hands shake so badly that she could barely hold on to her latte.

"Good Morning Sunshine?" She swallowed. "What do you mean, exactly?"

Mr. Grant shrugged. "It seems one of the producers has family here in town and got wind of your war of words with Fired Up in Lovestruck. They want to do a story on you two."

"How is that even possible? We don't even know who Fired Up is?" There had to be some mistake. She couldn't go on *Good Morning Sunshine* and talk about diaper craft projects. She'd never get a job in fashion again.

"They *like* the anonymity angle. They want to read some of the letters to the editor on air and do a short interview with you. At the end of the segment, they're going to call on Fired Up in Lovestruck to step forward and identify himself." Mr. Grant wagged a finger at her. "I told you people loved the chemistry between you two!"

Chemistry?

"Mr. Grant, please. I'm not sure this is such a great idea. Isn't it starting to seem less like a newspaper and more like an episode of *The Bachelor*?" Or God forbid, *Bachelor in Paradise*.

"Of course not. It's starting to seem like an episode of *Good Morning Sunshine*." He laughed, as did all of Madison's colleagues.

She didn't blame them, really. A segment on the most popular morning show in the country would put the *Lovestruck Bee* on the map. Subscriptions would go through the roof. Those Christmas bonuses that

Mr. Grant loved to pass out would probably be bigger than ever.

Maybe it wouldn't be so terrible. Perhaps once she had a chance to wrap her head around the idea, she could get on board with the hosts Samantha Williams and Meghan Ashley laughing it up over her lame attempts at parenting advice and Fired Up in Lovestruck's painfully blunt assessment of her maternal instincts. She just needed a little time to catch her breath and come up with a plan.

She also needed to come up with a killer outfit, because if she was going to become a national laughingstock, she was damn well going to look good doing it.

Mr. Grant clapped his hands to get everyone to quiet down. "All right, everyone. Let's get back to work. We still have a paper to get out tomorrow morning."

Right. One thing at a time. Madison's next column was only halfway finished, and she needed to get it turned in before she could think about her mortifying television debut. She turned to follow Nancy back toward their shared cubicle, but her boss tapped her on the shoulder before she could get very far.

"I didn't mean you, Queen Bee," he said. "You have a plane to catch."

Her latte felt like it was curdling in the pit of her stomach all of a sudden. "*Today?* I can't. I have a column to finish. I can't just leave town without any notice. I need time to prepare. I... I have my knitting class tonight."

She was grasping at straws with that last excuse, but come *on*. Mr. Grant would never throw her to the *Good Morning Sunshine* wolves without any chance to prepare.

Then again, maybe he would.

"Your segment is first thing tomorrow morning. You fly out of Burlington in three hours." He adjusted the knot in his adorably awful tie. "Get ready, Queen Bee. By this time tomorrow, everyone in America will know who you are."

In an unprecedented night of activity, Jack's shift had three overnight calls before his day off. The first two were ambulance assists—one for an elderly man who'd suffered a fall in his cottage near downtown Lovestruck and the other in a motorcycle accident way out on the interstate. The third was a three-alarm fire two counties over, in a town so small it was serviced by a volunteer fire department.

What started as an electrical fire in the attic of an antiques warehouse store spread quickly, and in the end, rigs from all the neighboring counties showed up to help. They'd managed to save most of the furnishings, but the entire building and all of its contents suffered heavy smoke damage.

Jack, Wade, Brody and Cap returned to the station covered in black grit and grime. Jack shrugged out of his turnout gear, peeled his T-shirt off and scrubbed his face at the bathroom sink before collapsing into one of the bunk beds. The wakeup bell was scheduled to go off at six-thirty—barely an hour away.

He felt like he'd just closed his eyes when the bell sounded, but he got up, swigged a few cups of coffee and filled out a report on the motorcycle accident in the half hour remaining before the end of his shift. Once all the members of the B team had arrived, he waved at Wade, more than ready to head home.

It was his off-duty day, which meant he'd get to see Madison later. *Finally.* Three days and nights had never felt so long before. She'd disappeared after their almost-kiss in the bathroom. One minute she'd been there, and the next, he'd looked up from the twins and she was gone. He'd had no idea what to make of it.

They'd shared something in that bathroom while his daughters splashed in the tub—something intimate, something important. He didn't want to ruin it by pressuring her into explaining why she'd slipped away. He just wanted to hold on to the memory of her face in his hands, the delicious ache that had come over him when her lips parted and the trembling softness in her voice when she'd whispered to him.

I trust you.

He could have lived on that memory until the day he died, but he'd realized something during the past three nights at the firehouse. He didn't want to live on memories anymore. He wanted to *live*, period. And he definitely wanted to finish what he and Madison had started.

At least he'd managed to convince himself that she wasn't Queen Bee. The asinine diaper article had all but settled that question. He couldn't imagine Madison writing something so ridiculous. She might not know her way around a shaker of baby powder, but he didn't think for a minute that she'd ever put Ella or Emma in harm's way. If that had been the case, he never would have hired her.

That diaper bedazzling train wreck of a column had been completely irresponsible. He'd *had* to write another letter to the editor. It was his civic duty, plain and simple. And now Queen Bee was the very last person in Lovestruck he wanted to waste his time thinking about.

He climbed into the driver's seat of his car—a dad van, because what else would he drive?—and checked his phone before cranking the engine. The night before had been so chaotic that he couldn't remember the last time he'd glanced at it, and apparently, Madison had been busy blowing up his phone while he'd been putting out fires.

He had three text messages from her, two missed

calls and a voice mail. Jack wasn't sure which to investigate first. The last time she'd been so anxious to get in touch with him, she'd tried to get him to fire her, so the flurry of notifications on the screen of his iPhone felt like a bad sign.

Up and down Main Street, the sleepy town of Lovestruck was waking up. Shopkeepers were opening their doors, and the usual morning crowd at the Bean hovered around the entrance, sipping drinks and making morning chitchat. In the distance, cool blue mist clung to the base of the Appalachian Mountains, making the horizon look like a watercolor painting. Jack took a deep breath and tapped the text message icon on his screen.

There's something I need to tell you.

That first message was enough to make him skip the rest and go straight to the voice mail. Her message wasn't any more forthcoming, though. She just said she'd had to go out of town unexpectedly and would see him later tonight for her regularly scheduled nanny shift. She'd call if she ran into unexpected travel delays and she apologized in advance for "anything that caught him by surprise" between now and then.

Jack went still as stone in the front seat of his van. He stared down at the phone in his hands, willing it to somehow provide him with more information. The screen faded to black, mocking him.

Anything that caught him by surprise...

What did that mean, exactly? He wasn't sure he wanted to know.

He tried returning her call, but it rolled straight to voice mail, so he tucked his phone away and drove home as the sun rose high in the sky, bathing the town in the glittering morning light.

Ella and Emma were wide awake, smearing mashed bananas on the trays of their matching highchairs when Jack walked through the side door and into the kitchen. They were both so immersed in pulverizing their breakfast that they didn't bother looking up when he entered the room. Likewise, his mom was glued to the small television he kept near the end of the kitchen counter for the occasional moments when he felt like getting caught up on world events or watching UVM football while he washed bottles or strained vegetables.

"Hello?" he said when no one seemed to notice him.

"Jack!" Sarah Cole flew across the kitchen, grabbed him by the arm and dragged him toward the television. "You got home just in time. You're not going to believe this."

He was dead on his feet, in no mood for perky morning programming and he could already see the garishly bright set of *Good Morning Sunshine* over his mom's shoulder. But when he got a closer look at the woman sitting on the pristine white sofa next to Meghan Ashley, he suddenly understood her sense of urgency.

It was Madison, right there on national television. She'd done something to her hair. It was sleek and smooth, falling over her shoulders in a glossy curtain, but he would have known her anywhere. What he didn't know was what she was doing on one of the most popular TV shows in the country.

The words from her text message flashed in his head like a neon sign. *There's something I need to tell you.* He was beginning to think he might know what it was.

"So, Madison, tell us why you've been writing your column for the *Lovestruck Bee* under a pen name." Meghan Ashley smiled from ear to ear as the bottom dropped right out of Jack's world.

A little bar that read *Madison Jules, Lovestruck, Vermont's Queen Bee*, flashed across the bottom of the television screen while Madison answered Meghan's question. Jack tried to concentrate on what she was saying, but his heart was suddenly beating so hard that a terrible roar pulsed in his ears. Letters were popping up on the screen—*his* letters—one, then another and another, until they filled up the entire space.

"Wow, that's more than just a line or two. This person seems almost obsessed with what you've been writing." Meghan pulled a face.

Jack closed his eyes. What was *happening*?

"I can't believe your night nanny is Queen Bee. I had *no* idea." Jack's mom shook her head. "Did you?"

He wasn't sure how to answer that, so he didn't.

Because deep down, he'd had a pretty good inkling as to Queen Bee's identity. He'd just managed to convince himself otherwise, especially after the diaper article.

Actually, that wasn't completely true. On some level, he'd known since that fateful day in the library when she'd dropped the truth at his feet. He'd somehow hoped he could wish it away, because he wasn't sure where to go from here.

You have to tell her you're Fired Up from Lovestruck.

He ground his teeth as he watched more of his words flash across the picture. Taken altogether, they looked so much worse than he could have possibly imagined. No wonder Wade had been worried about him. Now everyone in America would know what he'd been up to in his spare time.

At least they didn't know who he was. It was his only saving grace.

"Jack, sweetheart. Are you okay?" His mom eyed him with concern.

Say something.

"Fine," he lied. He wasn't fine at all. He was a mess.

She scrunched her face. "You smell like a campfire."

"Occupational hazard," he said absently, still mesmerized by what was playing out on his television screen.

His mother was only half paying attention, now that the interview was drawing to a close. She cleaned the twins' messy hands with a damp cloth and replaced their mashed bananas with sippy cups of apple juice. "Why don't you take a quick shower and get cleaned up before I head out?"

"Sounds good. Thanks, Mom," he muttered, reaching to turn the television off.

Maybe a blast of cold water could help him forget what he'd just seen. Then again, maybe not. Because in the moment before the screen went dark, Meghan Ashley had a special message, just for him.

"Fired Up in Lovestruck, come out of hiding. The world wants to know who you are!"

Chapter Ten

Madison slumped in the backseat of the taxi that was hauling her from Burlington back to Lovestruck after her *Good Morning Sunshine* appearance. The fifty miles was sure to cost a fortune, but picking up the tab was the least the *Bee* could do after forcing her to confront every single one of Fired Up in Lovestruck's insults in front of millions of television viewers. If she ended up staying in Vermont permanently, she'd probably need to learn how to drive. Lovestruck was small enough to navigate on foot or via her antique cruiser bike, but getting to the airport was another story. If she became an actual Lovestruck resident, she'd occasionally need to travel more than a handful of miles, and as of now, she couldn't even rent a car.

Wait. She frowned at the dreamy, mist-covered mountains through the car window. What was she thinking? She wasn't going to stay in Lovestruck. Staying had never been her Plan B. It had never even been her Plan C or D. Since the day Anna Wintour had oh-so-fashionably handed Madison her pink slip, she'd had one plan and one plan only: New York or bust. Lovestruck was nothing more than a layover.

She was just tired; that was all. It had been almost ten o'clock by the time she'd gotten all settled into her hotel near Times Square the night before, and her call time at the NBC studios this morning had been 4 a.m. Plus, she'd barely slept a wink. It was funny, really. When she'd first moved to Vermont, she'd missed the city noises of Manhattan so much that she'd resorted to using an app on her phone at bedtime. It had been weeks since she'd needed the wail of sirens and honking horns to lull her to sleep, though.

She blamed Ella and Emma for the fact that she now preferred lullabies and bedtime stories to ambient noise. As challenging as it could be to get two infants to sleep at the same time, there was something undeniably comforting about their soothing bedtime ritual. It was growing on Madison. A lot of things were.

She'd been dreading the *Good Morning Sunshine* segment with every fiber of her being, but the closer her flight had gotten to JFK, the more excited she'd been to set foot in her beloved Big Apple once again. The lights of Manhattan glowed beneath the airplane window like starlight, luminous and beautiful in the velvety darkness.

But she'd forgotten how gritty and overheated summer in the city could be. She'd forgotten how the rumble of the subway beneath her feet sometimes made her feel sick to her stomach, just like she'd forgotten how packed the sidewalks of Times Square always were. The simple act of getting from the airport to her hotel had been so sticky and exhausting that she'd found herself inexplicably homesick for Lovestruck.

And now here she was, sitting in the backseat of a cab on its way to Jack's house, glancing at the time on her phone every few seconds in anticipation.

Or maybe she was mistaking the tangle of nerves low in her belly for anticipation when it really meant dread. She'd tried to get ahold of Jack to explain the whole Queen Bee thing before he saw it on television, like everyone else. Naturally, he'd been too busy saving baby ducks, putting out fires and being generally heroic to answer his phone. Just as well, because she wasn't quite sure why she felt such a need to confess. He probably didn't care what she got up to in her spare time. She was his night nanny, nothing more.

Still, when the cab pulled up in front of his familiar, cozy cottage, her heart gave an undeniable tug. She gathered her things, paid the cab driver and tried to tell herself it was only jet lag. Because she couldn't be developing real feelings for Jack Cole. Likewise, she had no business gazing wistfully in the shop windows of the posh baby boutiques on Park Avenue, fantasizing about going on a full-on baby fashionista shopping spree for Emma and Ella. But she'd done exactly that after her segment had ended, when her time would have been better spent pounding the pavement for a *real* job.

"Thank you," she said, pressing a stack of bills into the driver's hand.

"Anytime. Welcome home." The older man nodded toward the overnight bag slung over her shoulder. "Let me get that for you, dear."

Welcome home.

An annoying little lump lodged itself in her throat, and she swallowed around it as she handed the driver her bags. She knew better than to argue with a Vermonter, and honestly, having someone care enough to haul her things and walk her to Jack's door wasn't terrible. Such a thing never would have happened in New York—not in a million years.

"Thanks again, I'll get it from here," she said once they'd reached the threshold.

The driver ambled back to his car and pulled away, leaving Madison alone to take a deep breath and knock lightly on the door, in case Emma and Ella were sleeping.

The seconds before Jack answered her knock were excruciating. For a moment she managed to convince herself that he'd been too busy saving the good citizens of Lovestruck—human and animal alike—from imminent danger while also caring for his infant daughters to watch *Good Morning Sunshine*. But it didn't matter whether or not he'd seen it for himself. The small town rumor mill had had all day to work its magic. Someone would have filled him in by now.

At last, the door swung open, and for an insane instant, Madison felt like throwing herself at him, which was ridiculous. She'd just returned from a quickie overnight jaunt to her favorite city on the planet, not a voyage around the world.

"Hi." She smiled a nervous smile.

"Hi," he said back, gaze flitting briefly to her partially smoothed-down hair. Her curls had started to spring back to life the closer she'd gotten to Vermont, as if they'd sensed her reentry into the land that had killed her best hair straightener. "The girls are sleeping. Come on in."

She could tell just by the way Jack was looking at her that he knew all about *Good Morning Sunshine*. He knew about Queen Bee and her war with Fired Up in Lovestruck. She may as well have been standing on his front porch completely naked.

"Sorry about the baggage." She nodded toward her overnight bag as she stepped inside, although the sentiment applied in myriad ways. "I came here straight from the airport."

He took her luggage from her, along with the pastel shopping bags filled with sweet little onesies and ruffled bibs for the girls, and gently set them down on top of a worn leather trunk he kept by the door. Ever the gentleman, ever the hero.

She suddenly felt like the biggest liar in the world. "Jack, I…"

"Madison, I…" he said at the same time, both of them talking over each other.

Then they both stopped and laughed. And Madison felt just like she had when they'd knelt beside the bathtub together, on the verge of something wonderful.

"I'm sorry," she blurted. She didn't want to stand with one foot in New York and the other right here, with Jack and the twins, when the here and now was beginning to feel far more important than anything else.

His eyes went dark, and he shook his head. As usual, she had no clue what he was thinking, but something about his expression made her heart clench. Maybe the fact that she was Queen Bee was a bigger deal than she'd thought. She'd expected him to be surprised, but thought they'd eventually laugh about it and move on. He'd probably never want to kiss her again, since she hadn't been exactly one hundred percent honest about who she was, but that was okay—for the best, really.

Almost kissing Jack Cole had turned out to be a massive distraction. *Actually* kissing him might be more than she could handle.

She bit down hard on her lip. *Stop thinking about kissing.* But his signature brooding expression was doing strange things to her insides. She felt all fluttery and warm, like she'd just been sipping brandy by a fire on a cold winter's night instead of trekking all over the Northeast in the dog days of summer. She averted her gaze in an effort to steady herself, but her attention snagged on the big wooden bowl of apples on the kitchen island and it reminded her of their run-in at the Village Market.

"Please don't apologize," he finally said, sounding oddly tortured.

The fruit in the bowl glistened like rubies in the

moonlight streaming through the kitchen windows. Madison couldn't seem to take her eyes off it, or maybe she was just looking for a distraction from this conversation, which had suddenly taken an awkward turn.

Funny, she'd never figured out why Jack needed so many apples.

She kept apologizing.

Jack had to get her to stop. He needed to just tell her the truth and admit he was Fired Up in Lovestruck, because he couldn't bear to stand there and listen to her say she was sorry when he was the one with so much to apologize for.

"I should have told you sooner," she said. "I actually tried a couple of times, and I know it must have been weird to see me talking about my column on television."

She had *no* clue precisely how weird it had been.

"So I really am sorry. I hope this doesn't…um… change anything?" There were questions in her luminous eyes—so many questions, and Jack had an awful feeling that the answers might break her heart.

"Please. Just—" he held up his hands "—don't."

Madison's gaze moved from something over his left shoulder back to his face, and she gave him a wobbly smile that made him feel like his heart had just been put through a paper shredder. "Fine. I'll stop."

He raked a hand through his hair, panicked at the thought of how to proceed.

It wasn't as if he hadn't had time to consider the wording of his confession. He'd thought of little else during the hours he'd waited for her to turn up at his door. He'd even practiced his conciliatory speech in between Ella and Emma's diaper changes and mealtimes. He'd figured it all out, too. He knew just what to say…

Or he *had*, anyway. Now that she was there, standing close enough to touch, words escaped him. He didn't want to admit that he'd been actively trying to sabotage her career since the day she'd begun writing for the *Bee*. He wanted to gather her into his arms, pull her close and tell her how much he'd missed her in the days and nights that had passed since they'd knelt beside the bubble bath together. He wanted to kiss her until her knees buckled, and then he wanted to carry her to his bed and show her how much the past few weeks had changed him—how much *she'd* changed him.

He felt like a man again. Not a dad, not a firefighter, not a husband, but a man—a man completely enchanted by a woman who'd swept into his life with her accusations of apple thievery and against all odds, had woken him up after a long, lonely slumber.

And now with five terrible words, it would all come to an end.

I'm Fired Up in Lovestruck.

He inhaled a ragged breath. "There's something I need to say."

She wrapped her arms around her slender frame as if steadying herself for what was about to come. "I'm listening."

"I'm sure you've heard about my ex-wife through the Lovestruck grapevine. Small-town gossip tends to go into overdrive when a mom walks out on her husband and newborn twins."

Madison nodded, clearing her throat. "I might have heard a thing or two…"

"I'd like to say I didn't see it coming, but that would be a lie. Natalie and I hadn't been happy for quite some time, and to be honest, when she left, I felt responsible. I'll always know that it's partly my fault that Emma and Ella will never know what it's like to have a mom." He looked away so he wouldn't have to see the pity in her gaze. He'd never wanted anyone to regard him that way, especially Madison.

Why was he telling her these things? Doing a deep dive into his most secret emotions hadn't been his intention at all. He never talked about Natalie—ever.

But maybe if he could explain what a mess he'd been, he could make her understand why he'd started writing the letters. Doubtful, but he'd already started going down that road and now he had to finish it.

"You know it wasn't your fault, right?" Madison said, her voice going all soft and tender. Jack was beginning to hate himself all over again. "Even if your marriage was over, she didn't have to leave those two little girls."

Jack nodded. His family and friends had expressed the same sentiment time and time again, but it was a tough thing to remember when he imagined all the Mother's Days in Ella and Emma's future—all the birthdays, dance recitals and Christmas Eves. As hard as he tried, he knew Natalie's absence would always be an open wound he'd never be able to fix all on his own.

"I wish it were that simple but it's not. What I'm trying to say is that I wasn't in a very good place. I was going through the motions and doing the best I could, and…" *I took out all my frustrations on a byline, and as it turns out, that byline was the one person I finally wanted to let in.*

His throat grew thick, and Madison was looking up at him, eyes wide and luminous, and he couldn't bring himself to say it. Not yet. "And then I met you, and things changed."

It was every bit as truthful as his secret identity, maybe more so. But she still didn't have a crucial part of the puzzle.

"How so?" Madison took a step closer and rested a delicate hand on his chest. It was the gentlest of touches, but Jack felt it down to his very core. "Tell me how things changed."

They were entering dangerously intimate territory, and even though Jack's head told him to stay put, his stubborn heart wanted to follow Madison right down that road of temptation.

"It got a lot messier, for starters." He made an exploding motion with one of his hands. "Baby powder everywhere."

She swatted playfully at him. "Very funny. We both know I'm far from perfect, but you refuse to fire me, so here I am."

Yes, here she was, and Jack couldn't leave it at that. She needed to know the truth—all of it, not just the terrible part.

So he touched a fingertip to her chin, forcing her to meet his gaze and with quiet sincerity, he said, "That's because I find all your imperfections utterly perfect."

"You do?" She rose up on her tiptoes, and suddenly her pillowy lips were within kissing distance.

"I do," he said, and it took every ounce of self-control he could muster to take a small backward step. But he still hadn't finished telling her what he needed to say, and kissing her now would make him the worst sort of liar.

Madison blinked, clearly confused by his sudden withdrawal. For a brief moment her face crumpled, and then she cleared her throat and pasted on a smile.

"Sorry, I…" She shook her head and let out a nervous laugh. "We shouldn't."

"Wait. I just need to finish…"

"No explanation needed. Truly. I mean, you're right, of course. This—" she gestured back and forth between them "—would never work."

Jack's mouth abruptly closed before he could manage to steer the conversation back toward his troublesome secret identity. He felt himself frown.

She thought they would never work?

"You know," she continued. "Because of the whole nanny and boss thing."

"Right," he said. The fact that she was his night nanny was just the tip of the iceberg. Madison just wasn't privy to that information…yet.

"Plus, you have a family to take care of. I'm not exactly mom material, as that horrible letter writer is so intent on reminding me over and over again." *Ouch.* "Plus, I don't even live here. Not really."

She was stumbling over her sentences, talking a mile a minute, which he usually found adorable, if somewhat difficult to keep up with. But his mind snagged on one tiny, significant detail that wasn't adorable in any way.

"What do you mean you don't live here?" he asked in a wooden voice he hardly recognized as his own.

"Well, I do, but I don't." Her eyebrows squished together like she was trying to make sense of her own words.

Join the club. Jack's jaw clenched. "I'm not following."

"I'm a fashion journalist. I'm just here working at the *Bee* and staying with my aunt until I get an offer to move back to New York," she said, sounding wholly unconvinced. Still, this news was an unexpected arrow straight to Jack's heart. "I guess I thought you knew that. I mean, it's no secret that I don't exactly fit in here."

His first instinct was to automatically agree since he'd had the same thought nearly every day he'd known her. But somewhere between nearly burning down her aunt's barn, reading *Vogue* aloud to his six-month-old daughters and all her ridiculous listicles for the *Bee*, she'd made a place for herself in Lovestruck. He couldn't imagine his hometown without her, but apparently, she had one foot out the door. Just like someone else whose departure had turned his life completely upside down.

Not all women are like Natalie, you know.

Wade had said those exact words to Jack on the very day he'd met Madison, and somewhere in the dark pit of his heart, he knew they were true. But he couldn't think straight in the wake of the bomb Madison had just dropped. His chest felt impossibly tight all of a sudden, like he couldn't catch a full breath.

She's right. The realization hit him with the devastating force of a five-alarm fire. *This would never work.*

What had he been thinking? That one near miss of a kiss meant he could let his guard down? It seemed laughable now. He couldn't do this. Ever. He couldn't invite someone into his life—into his *daughters'* lives—only to have her pull a disappearing act.

"I wish you would have told me you were only in Lovestruck temporarily back when I hired you," he said tersely.

Hypocrite much?

She wasn't the only one withholding information—he was still keeping the biggest secret of all. But what did it matter now?

It matters, you fool. You know it does.

"It's not like I've got fashion editors beating my door down. I haven't gotten a single job offer since I've been here, and lately I've been thinking that maybe…" Her voice drifted off as she studied his expression, and then she crossed her arms—a barrier between them. "Never mind. You're right. I'm leaving the first chance I get."

He nodded. "Great."

"Great," she echoed, and Jack wasn't sure which one of them sounded more miserable.

"You know what? It seems nice and peaceful around here." Madison cast a wistful glance toward Emma and Ella's room, and Jack's gut hardened because he knew exactly what was coming. "I don't think you need me tonight. In fact, maybe it would be easier if I go ahead and quit."

She stared daggers at him, but beneath the sudden fury in her gaze, her big doe eyes shimmered with hurt.

This was the moment for Jack to make things right, once and for all. If ever there was a time for honesty, it was now. He knew he was being unfair—dragging his past baggage around and dumping it at Madison's stiletto-clad feet. If he had half a brain, he'd fall to his knees, tell her the truth and beg her forgiveness.

He *definitely* couldn't let her resign. The last thing he wanted was for her to quit. He'd convinced her to stay once, and he simply needed to do it again.

But in the end, whatever ceremony of words would fix the mess he'd made simply wouldn't come fast enough. Madison Jules wasn't waiting around for him to talk her into staying this time. She grabbed her overnight bag, turned on her stylish heel and walked right out the door.

Down the hall, Emma and Ella began crying in unison, almost as if they knew.

Chapter Eleven

Dear Editor,

This is my final letter. Please let Queen Bee know she's free to write whatever she likes, and I'll withhold any future commentary. Any attempts by the Lovestruck Bee *or a certain morning show to identify me are entirely unwelcome.*

It's over. I apologize for any hurt I've caused Ms. Jules.

Sincerely,
Fired Up in Lovestruck

"Do you want to talk about it?" Wade said as he tossed a wet, soapy sponge at Jack the following morning in the front drive of the fire station.

"Not particularly." Jack slapped the sponge against bright red steel.

The two of them were on truck-washing duty while Cap and Brody had been tasked with the less envious job of household cleaning. There wasn't a fireman in the world who preferred scrubbing toilets and shower stalls to cleaning the rig, particularly on a sunny summer morning when a cool breeze was blowing in from Green Mountain. The flag above the firehouse flapped in the wind, and bubbles rose from the big bucket of suds next to the ladder truck, floating down Main Street in an iridescent parade.

It was an especially lovely morning in Lovestruck, in stark contrast to the less than lovely thoughts spinning round Jack's mind. And no, he most decidedly did *not* want to talk about it.

But Wade being Wade wasn't about to let it go. "I saw your letter in the paper this morning. I'm guessing this means you haven't told Madison that you're her secret nemesis?"

"Correct." Jack scrubbed hard at an invisible spot on the wheel hub. Couldn't Wade see he was busy? "Nor do I intend to. I told you—she's not taking care of the girls anymore. She's got her sights set on a big important job in Manhattan. There's no longer any point in setting the record straight. That letter was closure, my friend."

"Closure. Got it." Wade dunked a second sponge into the bucket and got to work scrubbing beside Jack. "It's kind of crazy that she turned out to be Queen Bee, though. All this time you've been writing letters to your night nanny. What are the odds?"

Jack sighed. He couldn't wait for the day when Wade found someone he was seriously interested in. And that day would surely come, even though for the time being, Wade seemed intent on dating every available woman in Lovestruck. Jack knew Wade, though. Deep down, he was a teddy bear. When he eventually fell for a woman, he'd fall harder and deeper than anyone Jack had ever met. Jack planned on hounding him night and day about it, turnabout being fair play and all. He knew his friend was only trying to help, but couldn't they discuss sports for once? He'd bite the bullet and join a summer fantasy football league if it would stop the Madison interrogations.

"It's an awful strange coincidence. That's all I'm saying." Wade covered his eyes with his hand and squinted at him in the sunlight. "Some might even call it fate."

Jack arched a brow. "You already did—just the other day at the library, remember?"

"That's right, I did. And that was before I even knew she was Queen Bee." Wade shook his head. "Damn, I'm good."

Jack couldn't help but laugh, despite the complete lack of humor in the situation. "Forget it, man. I meant what I said in the letter. It's over."

His heart was having a little trouble catching up with his head; that was all. He'd started dreaming about her again—the way she'd risen up on her tiptoes just to be closer to him, the way her soft, innocent eyes turned to liquid fire when she was angry or aroused, that perfectly impertinent little mouth of hers. Madison was a challenge—a puzzle he couldn't quite figure out—and God help him, it was one of the things he loved best about her.

The dream had seemed so real that he'd woken up, climbed out of bed and expected to find her down the hall in the twins' room, rocking his daughters to sleep. Then he spotted the empty rocking chair, and he remembered that the only thing waiting up for him in the dead of night now was a crushing sense of regret. Even worse, he'd finally opened the shopping bags that Madison had left behind and they'd both been filled with gifts for Emma and Ella from her trip to New York. She'd shopped for his girls while she'd been away, and he hadn't even been able to tell her the simple truth about who he really was.

He'd done the right thing, though. It was better

to end things now, before they really started, than to wait until her bags were packed for good.

"She's planning on leaving," he said quietly and focused all his attention on the soapy swirls his sponge made on the fire engine's surface.

He didn't want to see the look on Wade's face. Wade was the one person in his life who would understand just how the idea of Madison moving away would make him feel. It was a light switch flipping off. He'd barely even begun to allow himself to want something more with her.

And now?

Now he'd found out she was Queen Bee *and* that she'd never intended on staying in Lovestruck, both on the same day. It was too much.

Except if he was really being honest with himself, the light she'd somehow managed to rekindle in him hadn't switched off. Not really. It still burned bright, and despite his years of experience fighting fires, he had no idea how to extinguish it.

Wade grew still. Out of the corner of Jack's eye, he could see his friend's hand, motionless, as soapy water dripped down from the sponge in his hand and pooled onto the ground in a dingy gray puddle.

"What do you mean she's planning on leaving?" he finally said.

"She's only here temporarily. She never intended to stay. She had a big job writing for a fashion magazine in New York, and now she's just biding her time in Lovestruck until she can go back." Honestly, it explained so much, particularly some of her more questionable columns. Not to mention her shoes. He really should have seen it coming—of all the people in the world, Jack should have known.

"But there's no specific end date?"

"No," Jack said. He wished there were. The sooner, the better, so he could get his life back on safe, solid track.

Wade shrugged. "It sounds to me like you're getting all worked up about something that hasn't even happened yet just so you can avoid the real problem."

Jack didn't have to ask him what that real problem might be. He knew. The sight of his stack of handwritten letters splashed across his television screen was impossible to forget, as was the talk show host's parting words.

Fired Up in Lovestruck, come out of hiding. The world wants to know who you are!

"You might have a point." He cursed under his breath. He felt like he had a target on his back and any moment a television news crew might pop out from behind the nearest bush and shove a camera in his face. "But what if she does it? What if she gets the job offer of a lifetime and leaves Lovestruck without a backward glance?"

"I think you're asking yourself the wrong questions, man." Wade tilted his head back and looked up at the cloudless blue sky, then offered Jack a knowing grin. "What if she stays? What then?"

Mr. Grant and the staff at the *Bee* were so thrilled with Madison's *Good Morning Sunshine* appearance that they threw her a literal party. After the argument with Jack the night before, she'd sort of hoped to sneak into work the following morning, dash off a column and spend the rest of her day emailing contacts in New York. She wasn't sure how or why she'd let her job search completely stall in the past couple of weeks, but that ended now.

Jack had done her a favor by accepting her resignation this time around. Now she'd have plenty of time to follow up on the two measly Skype interviews she'd had since moving to Lovestruck and to send messages to the various editors she'd worked with over the years. Thanks to her *Good Morning Sunshine* appearance, people who she'd never been able to get on the phone might actually take her calls. The next time she saw Jack, she should probably thank him for letting her quit and reminding her where her true priorities lay. Truly, she should. And she would…

But first, she had to deal with the giant black-and-yellow balloon bouquet on her desk and a sheet cake decorated with a buttercream bumblebee and the words *Congratulations Queen Bee* spelled out in yellow frosting.

"You did good, Madison. I'm proud of you," Mr. Grant said as he juggled a paper plate sagging beneath a brick of vanilla cake. "All of Lovestruck is proud of you."

Madison doubted it. She could think of a couple exceptions right off the top of her head—Jack, for one. And her trusty old adversary Fired Up in Lovestruck for another.

"Thank you," she said. "I guess I thought you might be disappointed that it's all over."

"What's over? Oh, you mean the latest letter?" Mr. Grant waved his fork at her. "Don't you worry about that. You just keep courting him and he'll come back around."

"Keep *courting* him?" Gross.

Her boss shook his head as he swallowed a bite of cake. "I didn't mean it like that. Just, you know, write another article that might bring him back out of the woodwork. Everyone in America is reading the *Bee* right now. We have to strike while the iron is hot."

"Super," she mumbled, and then she slinked back to her desk and wrote some nonsense about the top ten humorous onesies on the market for infants while her own plate of cake grew hard and stale. She just didn't feel much like celebrating, and she didn't even

crack a smile at the number-one onesie on her list—
Party in the Crib.

The feud with Fired Up in Lovestruck had never
been her idea of fun, but now trying to lure him back
into writing a letter to the editor was complete and
total misery, possibly because she was beginning to
think that Jack hadn't done her a favor, after all. He
might have even broken her heart.

All morning she'd been timing her trips to the
printer just right, so she could catch sight of him
at the station across the street during his morning
equipment check. She took her pages from the printer
tray one by one and pressed the warm paper to her
heart while she craned her neck for the odd glimpse
of him going over the massive engine with a soft
yellow cloth, buffing it until it glistened like a shiny
red apple.

She told herself she was only acting like a creepy
stalker because she wanted to make sure Jack was
okay. It didn't take a genius to know why he'd re-
acted so badly to her casual reference to moving
back to New York. In that moment she'd reminded
him of his ex. She'd seen it in the way the color had
drained right out of his face, and the second the
words were out of her mouth, she wanted to reel
them back in. She hadn't even been sure if she'd
meant them—everything had been so confusing
lately.

But did it even matter why he'd gone so pale? He didn't want her in the same way she wanted him. He'd made that clear before she'd said a word about leaving Lovestruck. She couldn't believe she'd nearly tried to kiss him. How could she have misread the situation so badly? Jack had said some nice things to her, and she'd taken them purely out of context. After being his night nanny for just a handful of days, she'd gotten caught up in the fantasy of playing house with him and the twins.

And now it had stopped. She had her life back, thank goodness. No more sleep deprivation. No more dragging herself into work at the paper after taking care of infant twins for half the night. No more getting to the office only to discover she had spit-up on her clothes.

No more Jack Cole.

"You dropped another stitch, dear," Aunt Alice said, hovering over Madison's shoulder at knitting class later that evening. Toby stood at her feet, wagging his skinny little tail with just a puff of hair on the end and gazing at Madison in silent judgment.

"I know." Madison struggled with another simple garter stitch. Jack's mother was seated right beside her, and she wanted so badly to ask Sarah how he and the twins were doing that she could barely concentrate on her needles and yarn.

"Do you want me to fix it for you?" Alice held out a hand.

"No, thank you." Madison examined her sloppy baby bootie in progress. "I've grown rather attached to the idea of finishing this project all on my own, even if it's kind of a mess."

I find all your imperfections utterly perfect. Jack's voice rang in her head like a bell, and she had to bite down hard on the inside of her cheek to keep herself from tearing up.

Great. She'd managed to get through the entire day in one piece, and now she was going to lose it in front of Sarah Cole.

"I think you're doing a lovely job," Sarah said, looking up from her neat, even rows of knitting.

"Thank you," Madison managed to say around the lump in her throat. "I'm not exactly a knitter. I probably should have started with something more basic."

Then again, the only reason she'd joined this class was to meet some poor, unsuspecting babies she could exploit for her job. God, she was a terrible person.

Sarah offered her a sympathetic smile. "You're fine. It's not until we really challenge ourselves and jump right in that we realize what we're capable of, right?"

"Exactly right." Aunt Alice nodded as she took

her seat again on the other side of Madison. "And the more you try and control the outcome, the more trouble you'll have. See your nice section of stitches by the toe?"

She pointed her knitting needle at a few neat rows of loosely connected garter stitches in the middle of Madison's half-finished project.

"I guess that part doesn't look so terrible," Madison conceded.

"That's because you loosened your grip on the yarn when you were knitting that section. Are your hands hurting right now?" Her aunt arched a brow.

Madison's hands were indeed aching. "A little."

"You've got to let go, sweetie." Alice winked.

Madison glanced back and forth between Alice and Sarah. The other students sitting around the table kept on knitting, their needles making rhythmic clacking sounds that had become oddly soothing to Madison since she'd moved in with her aunt.

"Forget what the bootie is supposed to look like, and just go with the flow. Sometimes whatever we're creating doesn't turn out the way we planned. It might look different from anything we've imagined, but that doesn't mean it isn't good or valuable," Alice said, and then she stood to go help a customer who'd wandered into the store off Main Street.

Toby's ears pricked forward as if he was contemplating going after her, but instead, he trotted toward

Madison and rested a dainty paw on top of her foot. The sweater he was wearing today was lime green, and when Madison smiled down at him, she noticed a handful of gaping spaces between stitches. She wasn't sure if they were the result of Toby getting a paw caught in the material or just plain sloppy knitting...knitting like hers.

She sort of hoped it was the latter.

When she looked back up, Sarah winked at her and then turned her knitting around as she reached the end of a row, leaving Madison to wonder if they'd just been talking about knitting or something else entirely.

Chapter Twelve

Dear Editor,

Is *Fired Up in Lovestruck* a real person, or all
those letters I saw on television yesterday just
a publicity stunt?
   Fingers crossed, he's real and soon to be
revealed to the entire town.

Sincerely,
Curious in Lovestruck
Editor's Note:

   The Lovestruck Bee *is a newspaper
founded on sound journalistic ethics. Every*

letter printed in the Bee *is true and correct, as received by the Editor-in-Chief, Floyd Grant, including those delivered under the name Fired Up in Lovestruck.*

Dear Editor,

Then tell us who he is!

Sincerely,
Curious in Lovestruck

On slow news days—basically *every* day in Lovestruck—Mr. Grant liked to hold brainstorming sessions in the conference room. Never mind that the "conference room" was actually just a corner of the bullpen, next to the water cooler. And never mind that the conference table wasn't even an actual piece of office furniture, but a repurposed barn door. Madison was almost used to it by now. She sat and jotted down ideas for her column while the lifestyle reporter waxed poetic all the upcoming festivals in the area. Vermonters *loved* a good festival.

"Excellent. We've got plenty of material for the community page, but I'd like to see a few more news pieces. Maybe even some light investigative reporting." Mr. Grant glanced around the table. "Any ideas?"

"I have one." Brett Johnson, one of Madison's colleagues, raised his hand.

Mr. Grant aimed finger guns at him. "Shoot."

"Since you mentioned light investigative pieces, maybe we should seriously try to uncover Fired Up in Lovestruck's identity." Brett shrugged, and seemed to be avoiding Madison's gaze.

"What?" She looked up from her list of ludicrous ideas and shook her head. "We can't do that."

Brett shrugged. "Why not? That's what investigative reporters do—they investigate things and report on them."

Madison managed to refrain from reminding Brett that he wasn't an actual investigative reporter. His last article had been a play-by-play of the local school board meeting. "It would be wrong. Besides, it's been a few days since his goodbye letter and we still haven't heard from him. I think he's really stopped this time."

Mr. Grant nodded. "You might be right."

Madison breathed a little easier. She'd pulled out all the stops the past few days, even writing a story on preschool prom dresses and Fired Up in Lovestruck had remained stoically silent. If she hadn't hated him so much she would have been impressed by his restraint.

In any event, she had a feeling he'd been telling

the truth. It really was over, and soon she could put this whole embarrassing episode behind her.

Mr. Grant, however, wasn't ready to give up. "But without revealing his identity, there's no end to the story. We can't just let it fizzle out. The *Good Morning Sunshine* producer has been calling me *daily*, begging for information on Fired Up in Lovestruck so they can bring him to New York for a follow-up segment."

"Maybe we should hire a private investigator to try and find him," Nancy suggested. "No offense, Brett."

"None taken," Brett said, clearly offended.

"We can't out him against his will. We just can't." Madison wasn't entirely sure why she was trying to protect a person who'd made her professional life in Lovestruck miserable, but it just didn't seem fair.

"I agree." Mr. Grant nodded. "But if we found him, maybe we could try and talk him into coming forward on his own."

Madison frowned down at her notepad, trying to come up with an argument against this latest idea, but before she could, an ambulance flew past the window with sirens blaring. A few beats later it was followed by a firetruck from Jack's station. Her heart instantly went into overdrive at the thought of him speeding toward some kind of imminent danger—yet another reason why he'd done her a favor when he'd all but refused to kiss her. She couldn't handle being in love with a firefighter. It was far too stressful.

Since when do you think you might be in love *with him?*

She rolled her eyes at herself. *Since never.* It was only a crush. Hadn't she already admitted as much to herself? Once she had an offer for a real job in a real city, she could leave everything and everyone in Lovestruck behind and she'd forget all about Jack and his adorable daughters.

That was the plan, anyway. She just couldn't seem to get fired up about implementing it. Plus, she was having a hard time imagining her morning routine without sipping coffee at Alice's kitchen table watching her aunt knit dog sweaters while Toby curled into a contented ball in Madison's lap. She already missed Jack, Ella and Emma like crazy, and she hadn't even left yet. Even the thought of never seeing Mr. Grant again left her inexplicably wistful.

She glanced at his rolled-up sleeves and furrowed brow. There was just something so endearing about the fact that he tried to run the newsroom at the *Bee* like it was *The Washington Post* during the Nixon era.

He threw his hands in the air. "Is someone going to check the scanner in case those emergency vehicles are headed toward a newsworthy situation?"

Every head in the room swiveled in Brett's direction.

"Oh, right. Yes!" He stood, red-faced, and nodded. "I'm on it!"

Madison bit back a smile.

This isn't so bad, she thought. Until she could go back to New York, she had a life here in Lovestruck, and it was filled with quirky characters and a homespun charm she'd never known she was missing until those things had become a fixture in her everyday life. Maybe Vermont didn't hate her, after all. And maybe, just maybe, the feeling was mutual.

So long as she was stuck here, she just needed to try and remember that Jack Cole was *not* her problem, nor was she in love with him, despite the flutter that coursed through her veins every time she thought about him. It was wholly annoying, and she was ready for it to stop.

So, so ready.

"Mr. Grant, you were right!" Brett ran back to the conference table, practically hurtling over the office chairs and stacks of newspapers in his way. "According to the scanner, there's been some kind of accident, and one of the firefighters from Engine Co. 24 is en route to the hospital in Burlington."

"What?" someone shouted, and then Madison realized it had been her.

She flew to her feet, but had to sit back down

because she felt faint and dizzy all of a sudden. She couldn't breathe, and her heart was pounding so hard that she thought it might beat right out of her chest.

What if Jack was hurt?

Don't think it. She inhaled a shaky breath. *Don't even go there.*

"Any idea who it is?" her boss asked.

Brett looked down at something scrawled on the top page of his notepad. "A Lieutenant Jack Cole, but we can't release the name until the family's been notified of his injuries."

No. It couldn't be. Just…

No.

"Of course." Mr. Grant nodded. "We should probably send someone up to the hospital in Burlington to cover it, though. Are you up for it, Brett?"

Brett sprinted back to his desk to get his things together as Madison squeezed her eyes shut tight in an attempt to keep herself from crying. Everyone knew weeping at the office was unacceptable. It was just about the most unprofessional thing a person could do. She'd never even come close to crying at *Vogue*, but panicked tears were already streaming down her face—wet, sloppy, mortifying tears.

You're not *in love with him*, she reminded herself, but it didn't matter. Not now.

She stood on shaky legs. "Take me with you."

* * *

Jack's head hurt like hell, but nothing hurt quite as bad as his pride did.

"Is this really necessary?" He sat up in the hospital bed and gestured toward his flimsy gown, the sheets and the general surroundings of his private room. "I have twins. I need to get home."

"Lieutenant, you have a concussion with a small nonarterial bleed. You're not going anywhere." The nurse patted his pillow and then loomed over him until he relented and rested his head on it.

Ouch.

Lying down hurt. The soft, downy pillow hurt. *Everything* hurt, but wasn't a mild concussion really just a glorified headache?

He closed his eyes against the glare of the overhead light. "When can I go home? The girls need me."

"No, they really don't." The nurse's soft-soled shoes made squishy noises as she padded from one side of his bed to the other. "Your captain spoke to your mother, and she and your dad are staying with the girls. No need to worry."

Cap had called his mother? Marvelous. That was exactly the sort of drama he'd hoped to avoid.

"Can I call her?" he muttered. At least that was what he meant to say, but his words garbled together into one long slur. "She'sgoingtoworrrrrry."

"I think it's best you wait until morning. You're a little too groggy to convince your mom that you're fine right now. If she hears you like this, it could just make things worse."

Why couldn't he talk? It couldn't be a side effect of his pain medication, because they refused to give him any. He'd already asked for some…a couple of times. Apparently, it could mask the symptoms of a more serious problem, so his aching head wasn't going away anytime soon.

"Home?" he asked, because the effort required to string together an entire sentence was more than he could manage.

"The doctor has ordered another CT scan tomorrow morning. So long as there's no progression of the bleed, you'll be discharged. Until then, you need to *rest*, Lieutenant. Got it?" She pressed the call button into his right hand.

He cracked an eye open and smiled, but suspected it looked more like a grimace than any approximation of a pleasant expression. "Got it."

She jammed her hands on her hips. "I'm serious. Don't try and stand up on your own. If you need anything, just press this button and someone will come help you."

He nodded and his headache, which had begun to ease into a dull pain, throbbed to life again.

The nurse's expression turned sympathetic. "I'm

sorry you're stuck here, Lieutenant. That's what you get for being a hero. What are your twins' names?"

"Ella and Ella," he mumbled. "I mean Emma and Emma."

Why couldn't he get it right? Was he really groggy enough that he couldn't get his infant daughters' names straight?

"Yep, you're woozy, all right." The nurse laughed. "All right, hero. It's time for lights out. Don't forget—press the call button if you need anything."

He held up the button as a gesture of compliance and then let his arm flop back down on the bed. God, he was tired. He wasn't sure he'd ever been so exhausted in his life. Not even when the twins first came home from the hospital.

The door closed with a soft click as the nurse left the room, and Jack wondered how long he would have to wait for a different, more lenient caretaker to take over her shift. He needed a telephone, damn it.

His cell was probably still on the rig or back in his locker at the station if Wade had remembered to grab it for him. He moved his head gently back and forth, searching the room for a landline, but it was situated on the nightstand, which the nurse had wheeled out of reach.

He closed his eyes and sighed. He trusted his captain to keep his mom and dad calm. Cap was great at that sort of thing, which was one of myriad reasons why he was an exceptional senior officer. Also, the nurse had been right—hearing Jack slur his words would only upset his mom. Sarah Cole was as strong as they came, and she'd had years of being a firefighter's mother under her belt, but she would probably have strapped the twins into the back of his dad van and headed straight to Burlington if she'd heard him confuse Ella and Emma's names like he did just a few minutes ago.

His family was safe and sound. The best thing he could do for them was get himself rested up and patched back together so he could go home in one piece. They weren't the ones he was so anxious to call.

When Wade had stared down at Jack as he was being strapped to a gurney and hauled into the back of an ambulance, he'd asked if there was anyone else they should contact about his accident. Madison's name had almost tripped right off Jack's tongue. He'd had to grind his teeth together to keep from saying it.

Getting injured on the job had a way of knocking a firefighter's priorities immediately into proper alignment. Jack had seen it happen time and time again. He'd witnessed fires put an end to divorce proceedings, family estrangements and long-held grudges of all kinds. That was the unexpected, beautiful truth about fire—at first glance, it was licks of red heat and burning destruction. But deep in its molten yellow center, fire carried the promise of re-birth. Great swaths of forests that burned always grew back stronger and healthier than they'd been before. Jack liked to think it worked that way with other types of fire, too. He knew it did. He'd seen it.

And even thought it hadn't been an actual fire that had knocked him flat on his back on the side-walk outside Ethel Monroe's Lovestruck cottage, he'd felt his own priorities shifting before he'd even opened his eyes. And somewhere beyond the fog of pain, he'd seen Madison's face, like a dream or a mirage or some kind of angelic vision.

Wade knew. That was why he'd asked Jack if there was anyone else he should call. He'd either seen it written all over Jack's face, or he still firmly believed fate had brought Madison into Jack's life for a reason. He probably thought fate had thrown Jack out of the old maple tree and given him his current concussion, but Jack was fairly certain it had been Ethel's cantankerous Persian. It was a classic Fancy move.

Either way, he didn't want Wade to call Madison. Jack wanted to do it himself. He had things to say to her—important things…

If only he could get to the blasted phone.

Maybe if he just closed his eyes for a little bit, he'd wake up feeling better. Then he could make his way to the nightstand and dial Madison's number, except he didn't know her contact information. Her number was programmed into his cell, which was missing at the moment—at least he thought it was. Everything had gone so blurry around the edges after the fall.

"Madison," he slurred as sleep began to drag him under.

And then the bleeding in his brain must have caused an auditory hallucination, because he could have sworn he heard her voice, as soothing and lovely as the sweetest lullaby. "Yes?"

He dragged his eyelids open, and there she was, standing at the foot of the bed. Either that or his banged-up mind was playing tricks on him. He couldn't be sure. All he knew was that he'd remained stoic during the entire course of the day, even as he'd been hurtling toward the ground and thought he might die right there on the sidewalk, leaving his daughters fatherless as well as motherless, but the sight of Madison Jules in his hospital room—be it real or just a vision—nearly made him weep.

"Are you really here?" he asked, throat thick with emotion.

"I'm here," she said, and when her voice broke, something inside Jack broke along with it. "I hope it's okay that I came."

It's more than okay, he wanted to say. *I need you. I need us.* But he didn't have the right to say those things to her. Not yet—not when there were so many things that had been left unspoken.

"Of course it's okay." He attempted a smile.

Madison's face instantly crumpled, and it was only then that Jack noticed the trails of mascara streaming down her cheeks. She'd been crying... for *him*...even after the way he'd tried to push her out of his life. Even after she'd tried to kiss him and he'd taken that pathetic backward step away from her. Even after the letters.

She still didn't know about those, though. Even a concussion couldn't make Jack forget that very significant fact.

"I just..." She wiped a tear from the corner of her eye with a trembling hand. "I was at work and there were sirens and then one of our reporters heard from the scanner that you'd been hurt, and I just had to come. What happened? My God, are you burned?"

"I'm fine, sweetheart. It's just a little bump on the head. I fell out of a tree trying to rescue a cat named Fancy." He tried to sit up, but only managed to lift himself an inch or two off the pillow before he fell back down.

Madison's lips quirked into a half grin. Jack wasn't sure whether his use of an endearment had brought it about or whether she was amused by the reason for his incapacitation. He kind of hoped it was because he'd called her sweetheart.

"Of course you did." She rolled her eyes, but her smile grew wider.

God, she was beautiful—the most beautiful woman he'd ever set eyes on. Her smile could light up the entire New England night sky. And standing in his darkened hospital room, backlit by the hallway light streaming through the window on his door, her untamed copper curls almost looked aflame. She was fire, and even though Jack had spent his entire adult life putting out flames, for once he just wanted to give in and let himself burn.

Things that burn come back stronger and healthier than before.

Their gazes locked, and he swallowed hard.

What if she leaves?

As gingerly as he could, he shifted closer to the edge of the bed and patted the empty space beside him. "Come lie down beside me?"

She climbed into bed next to him, kissed his cheek and with her graceful body pressed against his and her hair fanned out on his pillow, just like he'd dreamed about on so many nights, Jack fell into a deep, peaceful sleep.

What if she stays?

Chapter Thirteen

To: MadisonJulesQueenBee@LovestruckBee.vt
From: AngelicaKentEOC@FashionistaMagazine.ny
Subject: Job offer

Dear Ms. Jules,
Your recent appearance on Good Morning Sunshine
was most impressive, as is your creative and whimsical approach to your small-town parenting column. I
particularly love your recent story on diaper bedazzling. It is my understanding that until recently, you
were a junior reporter at Vogue, and I'm pleased to
say that your fashion experience definitely shines
through in your work.

I would like to speak with you regarding a social media editor position here at Fashionista Magazine. Your familiarity with the high fashion industry, combined with your obvious knack for witty repartee—as evidenced by your correspondence with Fired Up in Lovestruck—would be a huge asset to our magazine. The position is available immediately and includes a generous benefits package, as well as a moving allowance. If you have any interest in relocating to Manhattan, please give me a call at your earliest possible convenience.

I look forward to hearing from you.

Best wishes,
Angelica Kent
Editor-in-Chief
Fashionista * where high fashion meets fun

The gentle vibration of Madison's cell phone in the pocket of her polka dot swing dress stirred her to consciousness just as the morning light pouring through the window of Jack's hospital room was shifting from pale pink to a pure lemon yellow. Her eyes drifted open, and even though years of putting her career before anything and everything else had her itching to read the incoming email, she paused to take in the sight of Jack's handsome face resting just inches from hers.

She'd spent the entire night in Jack's hospital bed. By some miracle, the nurse who'd come to check in on him every so often hadn't uttered a word of protest. She'd just offered a quiet smile and made an offhand comment about how nice it was to see Jack finally content. And weirdly, that was exactly how Madison felt waking up beside him: content. As if she'd finally landed in the place where she was supposed to be—not New York, not her feather bed in Aunt Alice's guest room with Toby curled at her feet—but tucked right alongside Jack where she could feel his broad chest rising and falling beneath the palm of her hand.

She'd been terrified the entire ride to Burlington in the passenger seat of Brett's car. He seemed to make an effort to tamp down his enthusiasm over chasing a news story that wasn't in any way related to a bake sale or a maple syrup festival, clearly sensing that she was upset at the prospect of Jack being injured. Upset was an understatement, actually. She couldn't stop thinking about Ella and Emma and what would happen to them if they lost their dad. Fate wouldn't be that cruel, would it?

She knew firsthand it could, though. Fate or destiny or whatever unseen force that had put Jack in the hospital had also been behind the death of her mother when Madison had been too young to remember a single thing about her. No one knew what might happen from one day to the next, which was precisely why her father had taught her to always be prepared. Invest in yourself and your future. Always make the smart choice, the *safe* choice. And by all means, think twice before letting someone get too close. He'd never exactly said that last part out loud, but the message had been there all the same. She'd learned it by the way he'd dote on her, but always somehow treat her like an adult instead of a child—by the way he'd kiss her on the forehead when he tucked her in at night but never said anything in response when she'd tell him, "I love you, Daddy."

She'd learned it by watching him choose to remain single until his dying day. He'd never once gone on a date or brought anyone home to meet Madison. Her father worked. He'd been married to his office, and according to Aunt Alice, he hadn't always been that way. His workaholic tendencies had only begun after Madison's mother died. It had been the way he coped with his grief until, ultimately, it became his way of life.

Madison understood him, though. And she'd emulated him the best she could, because it was what she knew. Her dad was a brilliant man, as smart as they came. She didn't date at all until college, and even then, she kept her boyfriends at arm's length. She had places to go, things to do and she didn't need the complication of heartbreak to get in her way.

But heartbreak had found her, anyway. When Brett announced that Jack was the firefighter who'd been taken to the hospital, it felt like the bottom had dropped out of Madison's world. She'd tried her best not to care about him—or his girls—especially after he'd let her quit. But it was too late. She'd apparently gone and fallen in love with him accidentally. It was the only explanation for the sudden and overwhelming sense of dread that had come over her when she'd found out he'd been injured.

So she'd gone to him, having no clue what sort of mess she'd be walking into or whether or not he'd even want to see her. While Brett tried to convince the firefighters milling about the hospital waiting room to talk to him on the record, she'd stood on the fringe of the crowd, willing her legs not to buckle beneath her. Wade had taken one look at her, grabbed her hand and led her to Jack's room.

"He's not supposed to have visitors," he'd muttered, then shot her a wink. "But I won't tell if you don't."

And somehow the scariest part of all had been the moment Jack opened his eyes and found her lingering at the foot of the bed. He'd said her name—or at least she thought he had. His speech was slurred and there was a bandage on his head, just above one of his beautiful blue eyes. All of Madison's hopes and dreams seemed to gather in a tight lump in her throat, and when he'd smiled at her and called her sweetheart, she could have sworn her heart cracked wide open.

Ten hours later here she was—waking up in his bed to find an email offering her a one-way ticket out of Lovestruck and back to her old life in New York. The best part about the job offer was that she'd never even contacted *Fashionista*. *They* wanted *her*, which meant she could probably write her own ticket. Instead of living with her aunt in rural Vermont, she could find a posh little apartment overlooking the glittering skyline of her favorite city in the world. She'd get to dress up in designer gowns and attend all the big shows during New York Fashion Week. Best of all, she wouldn't simply be a writer. She'd be an editor!

She'd have to be a fool not to slip out of bed, step out into the hallway and dial Angelica Kent's number right away. The offer was everything she'd been hoping for, but for reasons she didn't quite understand, hadn't taken the time to pursue. It was a life-changing opportunity.

But Madison suddenly wasn't sure if she *wanted* her life to change. At the moment her life seemed just fine the way it was.

Was that crazy? It had to be, right? She couldn't toss away her entire future to stay in Lovestruck just because she had feelings for a man she'd never even kissed. That was borderline insane.

"Hey there," Jack said groggily.

She tucked her phone back inside her pocket and snuggled into his side, all thoughts of Manhattan and *Fashionista* instantly forgotten. "Hey yourself."

Her heart pounded hard in her chest—not because it was weird waking up in Jack's hospital bed, but because it wasn't. It felt like the most natural thing in the world. *What* were they doing?

"How are you feeling?" She'd been so afraid of hurting him that she'd done her best all night to stay as still as possible, which in and of itself felt strange. He was so big and strong that she couldn't even wrap her hands around one of his biceps. If anyone seemed unbreakable, it was Jack.

No one was invincible, though, and Jack was a firefighter. He put his life on the line every time he went to work. Yesterday it had been a cat, but tomorrow it could be something much, much worse.

Jack propped himself up on one elbow so he was looking down at her. There was a fine layer of stubble on his jawline, and his eyes were heavy-lidded from sleep. But he was right there, so close, so very, very close, and he was still in one beautiful, unbroken piece.

"Never been better," he whispered, and then he cupped her face in his hand and finally—*finally*—

after so many near misses, he lowered his mouth down on hers and kissed her with a tenderness so reverent that it brought tears to her eyes.

She was crying.

Over a kiss.

She squeezed her eyes shut so he wouldn't see, but it was no use. Her tears spilled over, dampening his fingertips where they caressed her cheek.

"Don't cry, sweetheart," he whispered against her mouth. Then he made a slow, lazy trail over her bottom lip with the pad of his thumb, sending shivers through her entire body. "I'm perfectly fine and honestly, it was worth falling out of a tree to get you into my bed. I should probably send Fancy a thank-you note."

She laughed, and he pressed gentle kisses to her tear-stained cheeks. But suddenly, his tenderness wasn't quite enough. She wanted more of Jack Cole. She didn't just want calm and collected. She wanted the brave, burning heart that beat inside a man who wasn't afraid to walk through fire. She wanted the aching kind of passion that she'd never let herself experience with anyone else.

She wanted all of him.

So she balled the front of his hospital gown into her fist as their kisses grew deeper, needing something to hold on to—something to anchor her into this moment, lest she lose herself.

Too late, she thought, *I'm already lost*.

And she finally understood what Alice and Sarah had been trying to tell her at knitting class the night before.

You've got to let go...sometimes whatever we're creating doesn't turn out the way we planned. It might look different from anything we've imagined, but that doesn't mean it isn't good or valuable.

She'd made a life for herself in Lovestruck, and it didn't look anything at all like the life she'd had planned. It didn't look anything like the life the email in her in-box was promising. And that was okay.

Because right then, with Jack's hands buried in her hair and his bold, heroic heart beating fiercely against hers, it looked even better.

A soft knock on the door to Jack's hospital room put an abrupt end to the kiss Jack felt like he'd been waiting on for a lifetime. But that was okay—the kiss had definitely been the beginning of something, not the end. And he supposed he could tolerate the interruption if it meant he might be able to go home.

"Come in," he said, biting back a smile as Madison scrambled out of the bed and smoothed down her dress.

"Good morning, Lieutenant." The nurse who'd been looking after him since he'd first been brought to his room was still on duty. She winked at Madison. "And good morning to you, too, Ms. Jules. Or should I address you as Queen Bee?"

Jack's headache returned with a vengeance.

Somehow, he'd managed to conveniently forget about his alter ego since he'd fallen out of the tree and hit his head. Perhaps not *entirely*, but Fired Up in Lovestruck's antics had certainly taken a backseat in light of recent events. The respite was apparently over though, and all too soon.

"Please call me Madison." She let out a little laugh and shook her head. "It's so strange that you know who I am. Until a few days ago, no one did. Not even anyone in Lovestruck."

"Oh, believe me. All the nurses here know exactly who you are. We saw you on that morning show, and practically the entire hospital has been talking about it nonstop. Have you identified that big jerk who's been writing the letters yet? What was his name again?"

Big jerk? Jack coughed. The nurse glanced at him, but her attention moved swiftly back to Madison.

"Fired Up in Lovestruck." Madison rolled her eyes. "And no, we haven't a peep from him lately. Actually, the reporter who gave me a ride to the hospital last night wants to try and find him so he can convince him to come out of hiding. I'm just not so sure that's a good idea."

It was a *terrible* idea—the worst Jack had ever

heard. Thank goodness he wasn't hooked up to a heart monitor or else alarms would have been sounding all over the building.

He shifted in the bed, and Madison and the nurse both eyed him with concern.

"Oh, no. You're as white as a sheet all of a sudden." Madison's eyebrows drew together. "I thought you were feeling better."

"It looks like it's time for another neuro observation," the nurse said, pulling a checklist and a penlight from the pocket of her scrubs.

He held up a hand. "Ah, can it wait a second?"

He needed to talk to Madison in private. Immediately, even if it meant laying all his cards out right there in his hospital room.

"No, it cannot. The queen is right. You look terrible." The nurse glanced down at the checklist and back up at him. "Can you tell me your name?"

Fired Up in Lovestruck. What would happen if he just blurted it out? He'd rather do a slo-mo walk through a burning building drenched in kerosene. "Jack Cole."

The nurse checked off a box on her list. "And your date of birth?"

He sighed mightily. "Is this really necessary?"

"I'm going to tell you the same thing that I told you last night when you didn't want to spend the night here—yes, it is." The nurse arched a brow. "Your birthdate?"

"I should probably go. It looks like you have a lot going on here, and I have work in a little while." Madison waved a hand in the general direction of the door.

"No!" Jack sat up ramrod straight. Thankfully, his head felt much better this morning, so sudden movement no longer had him wincing in pain. "Stay, please."

She gave him a slow smile that built until it bloomed into a joyous grin. "Okay. I can probably stay for another hour or so before I have to head back to Lovestruck and get to the office. I'll just run and get a cup of coffee from the cafeteria while you finish up here."

And then with a flippy little wave she was gone, and Jack could only hope and pray that Brett wasn't lurking out in the hallway somewhere, armed with Jack's biggest secret.

He did his best to complete the neurological check in good humor, given that his nurse had looked the other way for his impromptu slumber party. He answered all the basic questions, sat perfectly still while she checked his pupils with her penlight and tried not to sigh while she checked his extremities for any signs of weakness, even though it felt like it was eating up half the time Madison had left before she needed to head back to Lovestruck.

Once he'd passed with flying colors, Madison returned and sat on the foot of his bed with her willowy legs tucked up under her and her hands wrapped around a steaming cup of coffee. She'd brought a cup back for him, as well, and while it didn't hold a candle to the Bean's maple blend, it wasn't altogether terrible.

"So did Brett stay all night? Is he taking you back to Lovestruck?" He tried to sound as casual as someone recovering from a head injury who was also hiding an appalling secret possibly could.

"Oh." She shook her head. "No, actually…"

"Knock knock!" A woman carrying a folded knit blanket poked her head in the door. "I hope I'm not interrupting?"

"Aunt Alice!" Madison hopped off the bed and waved the woman inside. "I was just telling Jack that you were on your way to come get me. You got here so fast."

Too fast—certainly too fast for Jack to unburden his fired-up soul. He felt guiltier than ever when he learned that the blanket in Alice's hands was for him, and she'd knitted it herself. Obviously, he couldn't ask her to go back outside so he could have a heart-to-heart with her niece.

Even if Alice hadn't managed to hit every green

light and empty expressway on her way to Burlington, he wouldn't have been able to spend any more quality time with Madison. Less than two minutes after Alice's arrival, a hospital technician pushed an empty wheelchair into his room and announced he was there to escort Jack to the radiology department for his follow-up CT scan.

But hey, at least once he passed this last test, he'd be discharged and he could go home. So he gamely got into the wheelchair and even let Alice fuss over him and tuck the hand-knitted blanket around his legs as if he were a nursing home resident.

"Do you have a ride back to Lovestruck once you're discharged? I'd be happy to come back and get you after I drop Madison off for work," Alice said as the tech began wheeling him toward the hallway.

Everything seemed to be happening at breakneck speed, and as much as Jack wanted to go home so he could hold his daughters tight and give his mom a good long look at him so she could put any lingering worries at ease, he found himself feeling wistful. He looked at Madison walking alongside him—*really* looked at her—and at that moment he would have given anything to rewind the clock and spend last night in a hospital bed all over again if it meant he'd fall asleep with Madison's head on his shoulder once more.

"One of the guys at the station is coming to get

me. Wade. Thank you again for the blanket." He reached for Madison's hand and held it loosely in his as they neared the doorway. "Assuming I do, in fact, get out of here, can I see you tonight?"

"Why? Do you need a night nanny?" She gave his hand a playful squeeze.

He wanted to laugh, but he couldn't. He didn't need a night nanny. It had taken finding Madison, stupidly pushing her away and being forced out of a tree by an angry feline for him to realize they both needed the same thing. They needed connection. They needed to love and be loved in return. What they needed most of all was each other.

He lifted her hand to his lips and covered it with a tender kiss. "No, I need *you*."

If only there wasn't one last thing standing in their way…

Chapter Fourteen

"No way." Wade shook his head, but kept his gaze glued on the steady stream of traffic snaking its way up the interstate toward Lovestruck. "Absolutely not."

Jack's CT scan had shown no progression of the bleed in his brain, so he'd been discharged with head injury protocol, which meant no drinking, no driving and no strenuous activity or heavy lifting. He didn't dare ask if toting six-month-old twins around counted as an overly taxing activity, because he couldn't wait to wrap his arms around his little girls and breathe in their delicate baby powder scent.

Nor did he ask if he should be going on a date in just a handful of hours, because he had a feeling that answer would also be a firm no. He and Madison would technically be staying in, anyway. Plus, he wasn't entirely sure she'd want anything to do with him *at all* once he finally told her the truth.

"What did you just say?" Jack said, turning to glance at Wade sitting in the driver's seat of the Lovestruck Fire Department's small SUV. His lingering concussion must have been messing with his hearing, because it sounded like Wade had just told him not to out himself as Fired Up to Madison.

"I said no. Don't do it, man. Keep that information to yourself." Wade sent a knowing look Jack's way to hammer his point home.

Jack leaned his head against the headrest and closed his eyes. "Correct me if I'm wrong, but you're the one who's been encouraging me to pursue a relationship with Madison since the day we responded to her hair-straightener fire."

"Correct."

"And now that I'm finally ready, you're telling me to lie to her." He shook his head. "Nope. Not going to happen."

Wade held up a hand. "I'm not telling you to lie to her. There's just no reason to bring it up at this late date. It's over. That last letter was your swan song, and you haven't contacted the newspaper again. It's done. You know what they say about letting sleeping dogs lie."

"True, but keeping it a secret would still be wrong." Jack swallowed. Why, oh why hadn't he just fessed up the instant he starting suspecting Madison was Queen Bee? "A lie of omission is still a lie."

"I agree, but you've waited too long. The window of opportunity has slammed shut, my friend," Wade said.

Jack tried—and failed—to tamp down his annoyance. This couldn't be good advice. "And when exactly did the window close?"

Wade didn't hesitate. He had an answer at the ready. "Last night, when you let her sleep in your hospital bed. Think about it, man. Telling her now would only hurt her, and I know you don't want to do that."

Hurting Madison was the last thing in the world Jack wanted to do. He'd already done it once, and it had taken a near-death experience to undo that particular mistake.

Still, wouldn't keeping such a terrible secret hurt her even more?

Jack sighed. "I might not have a choice in the matter."

"What do you mean?" Wade asked as he exited the interstate and steered the vehicle toward the town highway that led to Lovestruck.

Toward Madison.

Toward home.

"There's apparently a reporter at the *Bee* who's trying to track me down." Jack swallowed hard.

Wade's advice about the whole debacle was certainly questionable, but he was dead right about one thing—Jack had waited too long to tell the truth. If he'd fessed up weeks ago, he and Madison might have laughed about it…eventually. No one would find it funny now.

Wade frowned, thought for a minute and finally shook his head. "That's not ideal, but I stand by what I said. Keep it to yourself. If a hugely popular national television show can't find you, the *Bee* doesn't have a prayer. You're safe."

Safe?

Jack wasn't so sure. In fact, he had a feeling he'd left *safe* behind a long, long time ago.

Aunt Alice and Madison made it back to Lovestruck less than half an hour before she was scheduled to show up for work at the *Bee*. Toby scurried after her as she darted to her room, stepped out of the clothes she'd been wearing for twenty-four hours straight and tried to make herself presentable. The dog's tiny, quivering nose peeked out from beneath her discarded swing dress as she pulled on a pair of black high-waisted trousers and a pink-and black-striped blouse.

"Sorry, little guy," she whispered, plucking him out from beneath the dress and hugging him tight. His plumed ear twitched as she whispered directly into it. "Toby, you wouldn't believe the night I just had."

She spun the dainty little Chinese crested in a gleeful circle and then plopped him down on the bed while she finished getting ready for work. It was funny how drastically things could change in such a short amount of time.

She'd been wrong about Jack. He *did* have feelings for her. He just hadn't been ready to tell her how he felt, and that was fine. She of all people could understand the concept of self-preservation, and Jack and his girls had been through a lot. Of course he'd freaked out when she'd told him she was leaving Lovestruck.

But things were okay now. *More* than okay, actually. They had a date tonight—a real, romantic date—and she didn't mind a single bit that they'd be spending the evening at Jack's house with Emma and Ella sleeping right down the hall instead of going to a fancy restaurant or out dancing at one of the nightclubs in New York where her dates in Manhattan so often took place. In fact, she rather liked the idea of a cozy night at home. She just wished it didn't involve an injury to Jack's beautiful head.

Goodness, she really had it bad, didn't she? She couldn't wipe the smile from her face as she walked to work, and once she got there, she didn't even mind the fact that Brett had lived up to his word and thrown himself full force into his investigation of Fired Up in Lovestruck.

She poured herself a generous portion of hazelnut coffee into a mug emblazoned with the words Bee Amazing and wandered over to the barn door conference table, which Brett seemed to be using as his makeshift headquarters. Every letter that Fired Up in Lovestruck had written and sent to the *Bee* had been photocopied and blown up to three times its original size. The copies were lined up in chronological order, from one end of the table to the other.

"Any luck?" she asked, sipping from her mug.

"Not yet." Brett shook his head. "I'm thinking about bringing in a handwriting expert to take a look at his penmanship."

"Then what? Are you going to have every reader in town give you a handwriting sample for comparison and see which one fits, like Cinderella and her glass slipper?"

"Very funny." Brett straightened one of the photocopies a fraction of an inch.

"I'm only kidding. The handwriting thing is actually a pretty good idea. There are some distinctive pen strokes here, especially the way he crosses his z's with a little dash." She pointed to the letter where he'd used the word *puzzling*, drawing an invisible underline beneath the twin letters with her fingertip.

Then she frowned at the familiarity of the dashes. Madison hadn't thought about those distinctive z's in weeks, but she felt like she'd seen letters just like them recently. She just couldn't remember where.

"Everything okay? You practically floated in here, and now you seem upset," Brett said.

"I'm not upset," Madison said, taking another gulp of coffee. It tasted bitter on her tongue, though. Something wasn't right. "I'm happy."

So, so happy. She loved Jack, and she had a feeling he just might love her, too. She had nothing at all to be upset about…

Except she suddenly remembered where she'd seen z's like the ones in Fired Up's letter before, and unless she was mistaken, they'd been in the completed squares of the crossword puzzles on the end table in Jack's living room.

"Good," Brett said, but he didn't sound convinced. "I guess, um, just let me know if you think of any information that might help the investigation."

"Of course." Madison nodded, pasted on a smile and wandered back to her desk, where she spent the rest of the day telling herself she was only imagining things.

There was no logical reason why Jack's handwriting would have anything in common with Fired Up in Lovestruck's—no reason whatsoever. She was a journalist, not a handwriting expert. She'd gotten it wrong; that was all. There was nothing to be worried about. She had a perfect romantic evening to look forward to, and she wasn't going to let Brett's ridiculous investigation ruin it.

Nor would she let Fired Up in Lovestruck interfere in her personal life. Hadn't he caused her enough grief already?

But as the hours dragged until she was supposed to see Jack again, a slow burn of panic gathered deep in the pit of her stomach. And when at last she arrived at his cozy little cottage, she placed a chaste kiss on his cheek, then without a word of greeting, walked straight to the easy chair in the living room and inspected the stack of crossword puzzles on the table beside it.

Jack followed, watching her with an open curiosity that changed to an expression of masked alarm as she studied the lettering on the newsprint pages.

He cleared his throat. "Madison?"

The handwriting in the little boxes was an unmistakable match, even to her untrained eye. She noticed similarities beyond the cross hatches on the z's—like the way the closure of the o's overlapped, just like the ones in Fired Up in Lovestruck's letters. Brett had tried to tell her that particular characteristic was indicative of someone who liked to keep secrets, and she'd actually laughed.

She wasn't laughing anymore.

"Madison, talk to me, sweetheart," Jack said, and his voice should have sounded like the time he'd asked her to talk to him on the bench outside the fire station, but it didn't. There was a vague tremor of unease in his tone this time, and that was when she really knew.

It was him.

"Tell me I'm wrong," she whispered. *Please, please tell me. Lie to me if you have to. One last time. I promise I'll believe.* "Tell me you're not Fired Up in Lovestruck."

Jack just looked at her, and his blue eyes seemed bottomless all of a sudden. Two luminous pools of grief.

"I wish I could, but I can't." He pressed a shaking hand to his chest. "It's me."

Chapter Fifteen

Oh, my God.

Madison felt paralyzed. She couldn't move, she couldn't think, she couldn't even take a full breath. She covered her heart with her hands, and the crossword puzzle she'd been holding floated to the floor. She stared at it as she tried to take a deep inhale, but her head seemed to be enveloped in a thick fog of noise. Words that she'd read again and again were spinning in her mind faster than she could grab hold of them.

Bitter to the point of being inedible.

I must ask why a professional journalist insists on writing her material in this annoying list format.

Honestly, this latest attempt at journalism is so egregious...

She blinked up at Jack, trying to force his image into proper focus—trying to see him as the arrogant, judgmental troll who'd nearly sent her to the unemployment line before making her into a household name, famous for diaper bedazzling and terrible maternal instincts. She just couldn't do it. Somehow, he still looked like the man who'd knelt beside the bathtub with her and told her she'd make a wonderful mother someday. He couldn't be, though—not if he'd been writing letters to her boss all this time about what a disaster she was.

"I'm sorry," he said again, and the ache in his voice was unbearable.

Madison shook her head. "No. No, no, no."

She couldn't stop saying it. It was too unbelievable...too awful to think about, much less say it out loud. All this time, Jack had been Fired Up in Lovestruck. He'd been the one writing all those letters to the paper. He'd mocked her column since the very first day she'd worked at the *Bee*. He'd tried to get her *fired*.

Those things had been bad enough, but the really devastating part had been when he'd implied that she didn't care about children. She'd cried over that particular letter, because what he'd written had tapped into her deepest, darkest insecurities about her upbringing and her belief that growing up motherless made her somehow unlovable. Unable to mother. Unable to have a normal life at all.

Why did it have to be Jack that had written those words? Him, of all people?

"Madison, please." Jack's voice broke when he said her name. And the anguish in his tone brought tears to her eyes, which made her even more furious at him than ever.

She'd never cried over a man in her life, and now here she was, practically falling apart over the one who'd hurt her in ways she could have never imagined. What would her father say if he could see her now?

"Let me explain," Jack said. "Please."

"Okay, fine. Explain away." She crossed her arms and glared at him, trying her best to stay strong. Stoic.

But just looking at him grieved her down to her core. Those lovely blue eyes that somehow saw her in a way that no one else could suddenly seemed like the eyes of a complete and total stranger. And those hands—those big, beautiful hands that had held her so close last night had been the same hands that wielded her nemesis's pen. The only reason she could wrap her head around it was because deep down, this was exactly the sort of heartbreak she'd expected all along. It was why she'd tried her best to ignore the fact that she'd been falling for him since day one. Loving a person seemed to somehow end in loss.

Every. Single. Time.

She really should have seen this coming. There'd been so many signs, and she'd been oblivious to all of them—the piles of apples in Jack's grocery cart at the market, the strange way he'd acted at the library when he'd picked her books up off the floor and even the name he'd chosen: Fired Up in Lovestruck. He was a literal firefighter. How on earth had she missed that?

Because love is blind, she thought. She really, truly loved him. Much to her horror, she'd loved him all along.

"I didn't know it was you," he said, eyes going bluer than she'd ever seen them before. "I promise."

"Everyone in America knows I'm Queen Bee. You and I discussed it after I got back from New York, and…" Her voice trailed off as the memory of that painful night came back full force.

He'd told her she was perfect, and then he'd stepped away when she tried to kiss him. He'd let her quit her night nanny job, and all this time she'd thought it was because she'd done something wrong or he knew how she felt about him but he didn't feel the same way. But in reality, he'd been lying to her the entire night.

Maybe she deserved it. She'd certainly misled him

back in the beginning, especially about Toby. But *this*…this was a whopper.

"That night—the night I quit—you *knew*, and you didn't say a word. Is that why you let me resign? So you wouldn't have to tell me the truth?" She slumped down on Jack's sofa, because standing suddenly required too much energy. Trying not to collapse into a puddle of tears was using up every bit of strength she possessed.

"No, I pushed you away that night because you said you wanted to move back to New York and the very idea that you might leave—" he inhaled a ragged breath "—it scared the life out of me, sweetheart."

Why did he have to call her sweetheart? It made her go all swoony, even now. She looked away, because his expression was too raw, too vulnerable, for her to take. If she met his gaze, she was afraid she might forgive him, and she didn't want to do that. She liked feeling angry. It was so much easier than feeling heartbroken or accidentally falling in love with someone who could let you down when you were least expecting it.

"I just wish you'd told me," she whispered, but she immediately realized that wasn't quite true. What she really wished was that Fired Up in Lovestruck could have been someone else—some nameless, faceless stranger she'd never, ever met.

"I do, too," Jack said. "Believe me, I tried."

"Not hard enough." She swallowed around the lump in her throat.

If she'd known Jack was Fired Up, would she have gone to him at the hospital the night before? When he'd patted the empty space on the sheet beside him, would she have still climbed into his bed and kissed him silly? Would she have spent the entire night with her head on his shoulder and the palm of her hand pressed against the strong thump of his heartbeat, just to remind herself he was really okay, that nothing truly awful had happened to him and he wasn't going to vanish from her life like both her parents had?

Yes. She blinked hard to keep the tears at bay. Even if she'd known Jack had written the letters, she would have made those same choices—because she loved him, and love made people do foolish, self-destructive things.

Not anymore, though. She couldn't do this. She wouldn't.

And she didn't have to, because there was someplace else she could go—someplace far away, someplace she could start over and forget she'd ever met Jack Cole or his secret evil twin, Fired Up in Lovestruck.

Until that moment Madison had forgotten all about the email from *Fashionista*. She'd only opened it once and had neither responded nor called the editor-in-chief, as requested. The job offer was just sitting there, languishing in her in-box, but now it seemed like a lifeline.

She took a deep breath and thought about what taking a job in Manhattan would mean—more money, more prestige, a return to the glamorous world of high fashion. She could get her own apartment instead of living in her aunt's guest room and sharing a bed with a hairless dog.

Except staying with Aunt Alice had reminded Madison what it felt like to be part of a family, and she'd grown accustomed to Toby greeting her with a tail-wagging little dance when she came home from work. She'd miss the little guy. She'd even miss his goofy little sweaters. Deep down she had the nonsensical feeling that she might even miss Mr. Grant and the Main Street offices of *Bee*.

She chalked those feelings of unease up to nerves. The job at *Fashionista* was everything she'd been hoping for. Jack's accident had shaken her up; that was all. Finding out that he'd been Fired Up in Lovestruck all along might actually be a *good* thing—now she could walk away from Vermont and its small-town charm and never, ever look back.

"I'm going to go," she said, gathering up her handbag and bolting for the door. She stopped short of telling him that she planned on being on the first plane out of Burlington in the morning. The last thing she wanted was a long goodbye. "Give Ella and Emma a hug for me, okay?"

Jack looked as stricken as if she'd slapped him, but he took a deep inhale and nodded. "I'll do that, but can we talk in the morning? Please?"

She didn't answer him, because anything she might have said would be a lie and they'd both been doing enough of that. Instead, she forced herself to look at him one last time, because she knew if she couldn't meet his gaze, she'd never be able to walk away. But she did it, and as she looked into his eyes, bluer than blue, she willed herself not to feel anymore.

No more pain, no more love, no more fear. Instead, she let it all harden into a hard, protective shell of indifference. She was her father's daughter, after all.

"Goodbye, Jack."

This can't be happening.

Jack flinched as the door shut in his face and a lonely hush fell over his home. It was the sort of soul-deep silence that made him shiver, and for once he wished the twins would wake up so he'd have something to do besides pace around the living room tugging at his hair and trying to figure out how to fix the enormous amount of damage he'd done.

His head told him to stay put. He'd been down

this road before, and he knew where it led—nowhere good. It was best to let Madison go now instead of begging her to stay in his life only to have her announce she was moving back to New York a month from now or worse, a year from now.

Except the mess with Madison was strictly one of his own making. She was right. Heck, even Wade was right. He should have been honest with her from the moment he'd suspected she might be Queen Bee. Better yet, he should have never picked up a pen and written those letters in the first place.

Most of all, he should have trusted his feelings for Madison instead of fighting them every step of the way. He'd been so desperate to protect his heart and to protect his girls that he'd denied them the one thing he wished they could have—a family.

Madison made him want things that he never thought he'd want again. He wanted to slow-dance with her to the lullabies the girls liked to hear as they drifted to sleep at night. He wanted to stand beside her in the little white church on Main Street and make the sort of promises to her that would end with a kiss and a walk down the aisle, hand in hand. He wanted to write her letters, so many letters, with enough loving words to drown out the ones he wished he could take back.

He dropped onto the sofa and cradled his head in his hands. It was too late for those things now. He could feel it in his bones, and he had no one to blame but himself. Madison was gone for good.

Any sliver of hope he clung to went up in smoke when he turned up on her aunt Alice's front porch early the following morning with the twins strapped to his chest in their baby carriers. The sun was only beginning to peek over the top of the big red barn where he'd first set eyes on Madison Jules in her polka dot bathrobe. Daybreak swirled with fireflies, lighting the air like tiny sparks of hope. But just as Jack suspected, he was too late.

"I'm so sorry. She left hours ago for the airport in Burlington." Alice gave him a sad smile and reached out a hand to let Ella grab hold of one of her fingers. "What sweet little girls you have. No wonder Madison was charmed by them."

Jack's throat clogged. He wanted to ask where her flight was headed, but he couldn't seem to form any words. He also wasn't sure what exactly Madison had told her aunt about their relationship. Did he think they were just friends, that Madison had been his night nanny and nothing more? Doubtful, seeing as he was currently standing on her front porch, completely gutted over her niece's departure. Still, he wasn't sure what to say.

Isn't that how you got yourself into this mess to begin with?

The time for holding his tongue had passed.

"Please, come in." She held the door open wide. "Madison left something for you."

And just like that, his heart beat with his last, desperate shred of hope. His stupid, stupid heart.

"Did she?" Jack stepped inside, and a tiny creature came scurrying into sight.

The animal had a tiny tuft of fluff on top of its head and the tip of its tail, but was otherwise smooth and hairless. A sweater knit from bright purple and pink yarn hugged its slender body, and when it rose up on its hind legs and pranced at Jack's feet, Ella and Emma both kicked and let out twin delighted squeals.

"Is that—" Jack peered closer at the comical little guy "—a dog?"

It looked more like a character from a Dr. Seuss book.

"Yes, that's Toby. He's a Chinese crested. Don't mind him. He's ordinarily more shy around strangers, but he's a little out of sorts now that Madison is gone. Toby really enjoyed having her around."

The smile Jack felt tugging at his lips was bittersweet. "Madison mentioned that."

There's a three-year-old named Toby who positively adores me.

She'd looked so proud when she'd said those words to him weeks ago at the Lovestruck Bean. That glimmer of joy in her warm brown eyes should have been a hint that she didn't think she deserved such adulation, but he'd missed its meaning. Then came the talk at the fire station and that raw, unguarded moment by the bubble bath where he'd realized that the beautiful, beguiling woman who'd swept into town and stolen his heart feared that she was unlovable. And somewhere in the midst of it, he'd fallen head over heels for her aching vulnerability.

"Can I get you anything? Coffee? Breakfast?" Alice frowned at him. "How are you feeling? Aren't you supposed to be resting?"

"I'm fine." Physically, anyway. "Thank you, though. I just really hoped to talk to Madison before she left."

"I know, and I'm sorry. I tried to stop her. If that magazine wanted her to go to work for them so badly, it seems like they could've waited a few days, but she was so anxious to go." Alice sighed. "I guess Vermont just can't compete with Manhattan."

"I suppose not." Jack's head began to hurt all over again. He gave Alice a grim smile. "I didn't realize she had a job waiting for her there already."

"Neither did I. Apparently, an editor from one of the big fashion magazines reached out to her after her interview on *Good Morning Sunshine*. She didn't breathe a word of it to me until late last night."

Last night.

Jack's jaw clenched. Madison's sudden disappearing act was 100 percent his fault. She'd clearly gotten her new job offer before she'd come to his house the night before, maybe even before he'd been hurt. She hadn't said a word about it, though.

Could that possibly mean she'd had no intention of taking the job until she'd found out he was Fired Up in Lovestruck?

He hadn't thought he could feel any worse about her sudden departure until right then.

"Let me go get that gift she left for you." Alice held up a finger. "I'll be right back."

She bustled toward the hallway leading to the back of the farmhouse, and Jack waited, absently running his fingertips over the tops of the twins' soft heads.

"Dada," Emma said, and his heart nearly cracked in two.

Toby's fanciful head cocked to one side, and he narrowed his gaze at Jack. It was almost as if he knew Jack was the reason his beloved Madison had flitted off to New York and left everyone behind. Either that or Jack was losing it. Possibly both.

"It's my fault, I know," Jack said, and the little dog's plumed ears pricked forward. "I'm sorry."

Toby blinked at him a few times and then walked toward a big Vermont-flannel plaid dog bed tucked by the hearth, turned three careful circles on it and then plopped down with a sigh. Apology not accepted, apparently.

Jack couldn't blame him. It would be a long, lonely while before he forgave himself. If ever.

He shifted from one foot to the other while he waited for Alice, wondering if there was any chance her flight hadn't taken off yet. How fast could he get to the airport? Granted, he wasn't supposed to be driving at all, much less all the way to Burlington. Maybe he could get one of the guys to drive him up there in the rig. At least they'd arrive in a hurry.

"Here we go." Alice returned carrying a small paper bag with a whimsical illustration of a ball of yarn on it. The yarn unspooled to spell out the words *Main Street Yarn*.

"A gentle warning—they're not pretty. But Madison worked really hard on them." She offered Jack the bag, and he took it. "I loved having her in class. For a while there, I was kind of hoping she might stay here in Lovestruck and take over the shop someday. She loves fashion so much, and she's just a beginner now, but she could create some really beautiful things if she stuck with knitting. I guess it's just not mean to be."

"I suppose not," Jack said, clutching the bag.

He was almost afraid to look inside. He was barely hanging on as it was, and he really didn't want to start weeping right there in front of Madison's aunt and a clearly unhappy Toby. But Alice made no move to usher him toward the door, so he didn't have much of a choice.

He peered over the top of the twins' heads, reached into the bag and pulled out a lump of pink yarn. At first, he wasn't sure what he was looking at, but once he untangled the pieces, he realized he was holding four tiny, hand-knitted baby booties in his hands. Two pairs—one for Ella and one for Emma.

"Remember, it's the thought that counts," Alice said, arching a brow.

Jack guessed the knowing look she tossed his direction was a reference to the uneven rows of stitches and the way all four booties seemed to vary in size. He couldn't have cared less about any of those details. In fact, he preferred them this way. He could see what a struggle the project had been for her, and the fact that she hadn't given up made his heart feel like it was being squeezed in a vise.

Perfectly imperfect.

Just like her. Just like Madison.

When he looked up and met Alice's gaze, her eyes were filled with unshed tears. She gave him a watery smile. Maybe she knew what had happened between him and Madison, after all. Or maybe she simply missed her niece. Either way, Jack felt the invisible vise around his heart tighten another notch or so.

He offered her his best attempt at a smile, but could feel his face refusing to cooperate. What now? Where did he go from here? "They're perfect."

Chapter Sixteen

Dear Editor,

First Fired Up in Lovestruck disappeared, and now Queen Bee?
    Bring her back!

Sincerely,
Disappointed in Lovestruck

Dear Editor,

Lovestruck adores Queen Bee. I can't believe Fired Up drove her away.

Sincerely,
Angry in Lovestruck

Dear Editor,

I always thought Fired Up in Lovestruck and
Queen Bee were perfect for each other, like
two sides of the same coin.
I guess I was wrong.

Sincerely,
Heartbroken in Lovestruck

The entire town blamed Jack for the sudden disappearance of Queen Bee's column. Technically, they blamed Fired Up in Lovestruck, but Jack and his alter ego were one and the same, even if he still hadn't come forward and identified himself.

What possible purpose would that serve now? Madison was gone. Nearly a week had passed since he'd shown up at her aunt's house, hoping to fix things between them. He was certain Alice would have mentioned it to her. Even if she hadn't, there'd been enough unanswered calls and text messages for Jack to get the message loud and clear.

It's over. He'd written those same words in his final letter to the *Bee*—he just hadn't realized they'd eventually turn out to be so prophetic.

"Welcome back." Cap looked up from the newspaper in his hands as Jack walked into the firehouse kitchen on his first day back on the job after his concussion. "How's the head?"

Jack did his best not to grimace at the sight of the *Lovestruck Bee*'s banner running across the top of the front page. If he never saw another copy of the local paper again, it would still be too soon.

"Better, thanks." He glanced around. He'd expected to find Wade and Brody filling the other seats at the table, going over the paperwork from the prior shift, but they were nowhere to be seen. "Where is everyone?"

"Wade and Brody just took the ladder truck out to the elementary school for a fire drill." Cap folded the newspaper into a neat square.

Jack couldn't help catching a glimpse of his alter ego's name above the fold. Readers were still writing letters filled with questions about him and Queen Bee. He wished everyone would just let it go. Maybe then he'd have a prayer of doing so himself.

"While it's just the two of us, there's something I need to say." Cap leveled his gaze at Jack. "So long as your doctor says you're good to go, you're welcome to come back to work, but I want you to think about it—really think—is this where you want to be right now? Or is there something else you need to take care of first?"

Jack lowered himself into the chair opposite Cap. Clearly, he needed to be sitting down for this discussion. "I'm not sure what you're talking about."

A lie. Of course he knew. He just wasn't sure how Cap had managed to find out about him and Madison, unless Wade had said something. That didn't sound like Wade, though. He was nosy as hell, but he was also a trustworthy friend.

"Don't you?" Cap's eyebrows rose, and he gave the Letters to the Editor section of the *Bee* a purposeful tap with his pointer finger.

Jack closed his eyes and concentrated on breathing in and out for a moment before opening them and facing the look of disapproval on his boss's face. "How long have you known?"

"Since the very first letter from Fired Up in Lovestruck. It was rather obvious, don't you think?"

The next time Jack took on a secret identity, he really needed to choose a more subtle name—except there wouldn't be a next time. Ever.

"Why didn't you say anything?" he asked.

Cap shrugged. "It was pretty clear you were working through something, and the letters seemed harmless enough at the time."

Jack felt sick. He'd thought the same thing, and he'd been wrong. So very wrong.

"But that doesn't seem to be the case anymore," Cap said, sounding more like a concerned dad than his supervisor. Engine Company 24 was a family, after all.

"It's not. I've hurt Queen Bee—Madison—quite deeply." Jack swallowed around the sudden thickness in his throat. He kept thinking that moving on would get easier, but so far it hadn't.

The longer he spent without seeing Madison, the more difficult it became.

"I'm sure that's not an easy thing to admit, but I wasn't talking about Madison. I was talking about *you*." Cap gave Jack a sad smile. "I care about you, son. You've been part of this company and my life long enough for me to know when you're hurting. If you care about Madison the way I suspect that you do, don't you owe it to yourself and your girls to try and make things right?"

"I have—several times. Every day, if you want to know the truth." Jack closed his eyes and pressed hard on his eyelids with his fingertips to try and erase the memory of Madison's expression when she'd discovered the truth. The look on her face right then had nearly killed him, and he couldn't seem to be able to shut his eyes without revisiting that moment again and again. "She doesn't want to talk to me. Frankly, I don't blame her."

He felt like he'd wasted the last few minutes he'd spent with her. He hadn't shut up about the stupid letters. He'd thought if he explained how lost and miserable he'd been back when he'd started writing them, he could somehow make her understand, but now he knew that had been a grave mistake. If only he could live those moments over again, he wouldn't spend them talking about the *Lovestruck Bee* or Fired Up in Lovestruck or Queen Bee. Instead, he'd tell Madison exactly how he felt about her, because somehow he'd never gotten around to saying what mattered most of all—he was in love with her with his whole heart.

"She doesn't want to talk to you," Cap repeated. Then he snorted and said, "So?"

Jack opened his eyes and frowned at him. *So?* That was the sum total of his captain's words of wisdom? *"What's that supposed to mean, exactly?"*

"She might not want to talk to you, and I respect that. But there are other ways of making your feelings known." Cap cast a meaningful glance at the paper. "You've managed to do a pretty good job of it thus far."

Jack shook his head. He couldn't write another letter to the paper. He was finished with that—100 percent done. "Somehow I don't think writing to the *Bee* would get me back into Madison's good graces. Even if I wanted to, she'd probably never see it. She's gone back to New York."

"Then it sounds like you need to think bigger," Cap said.

Easier said than done.

Jack stood and headed for the coffeemaker. He was far too under-caffeinated for this particular conversation.

But as he made his way toward the kitchen counter, his attention snagged on the reflection in the darkened flat-screen television hanging above the kitchen table, just over Cap's head. A wooden bowl of apples on the countertop glimmered in the screen as if it were a darkened mirror.

Jack stopped in his tracks as a tiny flicker of something stirred deep inside his gut—something that felt an awful lot like hope.

"What?" Cap said, gaze flitting from the bowl of fruit to the television and back.

"You're a genius." Jack smiled his first real smile in a week. He grabbed an apple from the bowl and pointed at Cap with it. "Also, I'm going to need the rest of the day off."

Think bigger indeed.

Madison's feet ached almost as much as her heart did.

When she'd lived in Lovestruck, she'd walked pretty much everywhere in her trademark stilettos, and she'd been just fine. But setting her Jimmy Choo shoes back in Manhattan had been another story. Maybe it was all the steps leading up to the fourth floor walk-up she'd arranged to sublet from one of her old friends at *Vogue* who'd be gone to Paris Fashion Week for ten days, or maybe it was simply that everyone in the city walked at a much faster clip than they did in Vermont. Madison wasn't sure. All she knew was that she'd been back in the Big Apple for less than a week and her heels were raw and bloodied.

Plus, she was so out of practice using a hair straightener that she'd already burned herself three times—most recently on the thumb of her right hand, which was wreaking havoc with her ability to tweet, Snapchat, Insta and post to all the other myriad social media outlets that she was responsible for in her new position.

New York hates me.

She stared blankly at the glass brick walls of her cubicle. Madison didn't really believe New York hated her, but she was beginning to come to terms with a most inconvenient truth—the lifelong love affair she'd had with Manhattan just didn't feel the same anymore. She'd gotten used to moseying down Main Street and sipping her maple latte on the way to work in the morning instead of cramming herself into the subway and jostling for sidewalk space. She missed waking up with a hairless dog curled up beside her and the clickety-clack of Aunt Alice's knitting needles late into the night. Most of all, she missed Jack.

She missed him so much that she'd begun

Googling the Lovestruck Fire Department's webpage multiple times a day just to see his face. She'd gaze wistfully at his headshot until her cubicle mate—Felicity, *Fashionista*'s assistant beauty editor—would clear her throat, reminding Madison that she was supposed to be tweeting about the cape dress that Meghan Markle had just worn instead of daydreaming about the fireman she'd left behind.

"Who is he, exactly?" Felicity asked as she sashayed into their tiny shared space early Monday morning.

Madison blinked. She'd been daydreaming about her life back in Lovestruck—*again*—and hadn't realized Jack's chiseled features were lighting up her browser.

"Oh, um. No one, really." She jammed at the escape key until he disappeared and the hot pink *Fashionista* logo took the place of his strong jaw and dreamy blue eyes.

"I just thought I'd ask since you've looked at his picture so much in the four days you've worked here." Felicity winked at her as she lowered herself into her chair. Her lipstick was the same color as Jack's fire engine, and the Chanel jumpsuit she had on probably cost more than Main Street Yarn made in an entire month. "Not that I blame you. He's certainly hunky."

"You should see his little girls. They're six-month-old twins." Madison wondered how long she'd remember Emma and Ella's tiny little toes, their baby-soft scents and the impossible softness of their skin. She couldn't imagine ever forgetting those tiny details.

"Twins?" Felicity's perfectly lined eyes widened. "Wow. That's sweet, but I'm not really a baby person."

Madison nodded. "I get it."

She *did* get it, even though she found it slightly odd that Felicity kept a framed photo of an infant on her desk, despite not being a baby person. But everything else about Felicity screamed fashion plate, and there were dozens of other items on her desk that were completely non-baby related—a carefully curated collection of perfume bottles from Jo Malone, candid pictures from Fashion Week, no less than four engraved lipstick cases from Guerlain Paris. Madison couldn't imagine a baby in the pretty woman's arms, no matter how hard she tried.

Not that she was judging her in any way. Quite the contrary, actually. Just a month or so ago, Madison had *been* Felicity, and it was a perfectly wonderful way to be. Madison had been happy back then. Content. But then she'd gotten fired, moved to Lovestruck and now everything had changed. *She'd* changed, and now she wasn't so sure she belonged at a place like *Fashionista* anymore.

Every time she stepped off the elevator into the sleek lobby, she wondered what was going on at the

Bee. Had Brett finally found an investigative piece to work on, or was he still working the maple syrup and bake sale beat? What new recipes had Nancy whipped up for her food column? Was Mr. Grant still rocking his awful brown tie?

Most of all, though, she wondered if she'd made a mistake when she'd refused to forgive Jack for not telling her sooner that he'd been writing the letters from Fired Up in Lovestruck. She told herself repeatedly that she'd done the right thing, but it was getting harder and harder to remember exactly why she'd been so hurt and angry with him. She hadn't been 100 percent truthful, either—certainly not in the beginning. The letters Jack had written hadn't exactly been complimentary, but they hadn't been downright cruel, either. What was that old saying about sticks and stones?

Words will never hurt me.

Her heart wrenched. Jack's words *had* hurt her. She wished they hadn't, but they had. More than anything, she wished there was a way for him to take those words back.

"I'm off to the break room for a pressed juice. Want me to bring anything back for you?" Felicity lingered at the entrance to their cubicle.

"No, I'm good. Thank you, though." Madison forced herself to smile, and once Felicity was gone, she redirected her attention to actual work.

She posted a few snaps of various leopard print shoes and had just started crafting a graphic with shopping links on how to get Reese Witherspoon's latest red carpet look for less when Felicity came flying back to the cubicle, pressed juice sloshing everywhere.

"Madison!" There was a blob of green liquid right in the center of her jumpsuit's bodice, but Felicity either didn't notice or she didn't care.

Alarm bells started ringing in Madison's mind. They sounded suspiciously like the sirens on one of the LFD engines. "What's wrong?"

Felicity shook her head, and her glossy blond hair swished around her slender shoulders like she was in a shampoo commercial. The beauty department always managed to get its hands on the best hair products. "Nothing's wrong. But you need to get up and come to the break room. That fireman whose picture you're always staring at is on television!"

Madison's entire body went wooden all of a sudden. Jack was on *television*?

Felicity plunked her juice down on her desk and tugged on the sleeve of Madison's sweater—the fuzzy, hand-knitted one Aunt Alice had given her to wear to her night nanny job. She couldn't quite force herself to give it up, even though it was wholly out of place at *Fashionista.* "Come *on* or you're going to miss it!"

Madison stumbled to her feet and let Felicity drag

her toward the room. The closer they got, the faster Madison's blistered feet seemed to carry her. By the time she burst through the doors of the break room, she'd passed Felicity and was panting from the effort, even though she wouldn't quite let herself believe that Jack was really on TV. Not *her* Jack. He would never. Thus far, he hadn't even publicly admitted he was Fired Up in Lovestruck. Not as far as she knew, anyway.

But as she came to a skidding halt in front of the flat screen beside the coffee and juice bar, she was stunned to discover Felicity had been right.

"See, I told you!" Felicity waved a perfectly manicured hand at the television.

Jack was sitting on the infamous *Good Morning Sunshine* sofa, right where Madison had been less than two weeks ago. He looked so good that Madison felt like weeping at the sight of him, but what on earth was he doing?

Then her gaze shifted to Meghan Ashley sitting beside him, holding up a copy of the *Lovestruck Bee*. Oh, God, had they somehow identified Jack as Fired Up in Lovestruck and tricked him into making an appearance on the show? Maybe they'd told him they wanted him to come on air to talk about fire safety or something. He was dressed in his LFD shirt and the dark cargo pants he usually wore when he was on duty. It looked like he'd just slid down a fireman's pole and landed on Meghan Ashley's sofa.

Her stomach churned. Jack would probably think she'd called the station and told them exactly where to find Fired Up. Any and all hope they might have for a future was about to go up in smoke, no pun intended.

But you don't want *a future with Jack Cole, remember?*

A few editorial assistants who'd been busy pouring coffee joined Madison and Felicity where they stood, eyes glued to the screen.

"Who's that?" one of them asked. "He's hot."

Felicity answered before Madison could say anything. It seemed she'd lost the ability to form words. "He's Madison's secret boyfriend."

Madison shook her head in protest. "He's really…" *Not.* He wasn't her secret boyfriend and never had been. But she couldn't bring herself to say such a thing out loud, because that would make it real, and there was still a tiny, pathetic part of herself that refused to give up hope.

She just couldn't believe *Good Morning Sunshine* had dragged him on air, but it was the only explanation. Meghan was reading all the letters between Fired Up and Queen Bee out loud while Jack sat beside her, as stoic as ever. Madison couldn't imagine what was going through his head. The Jack Cole she knew would never, ever want his personal business broadcast all over the country like this.

But then the craziest thing happened.

After Meghan read Fired Up's most recent letter to the *Bee*, she turned toward Jack and smiled. He smiled right back at her before turning his charismatic grin toward the camera. All at once, it seemed as if he was looking right at Madison, straight to the most hidden part of her soul.

A thousand butterflies took flight deep in her belly, just like they had when Jack had reached for her hand and held it to the wall on the day they'd met. The question he'd asked her back then whirled in her mind.

Feel anything?

Yes, she wanted to say. *I feel you, and I love you... still.*

A banner flashed across the bottom of the screen, directly beneath Jack's face.

Jack Cole from Lovestruck, Vermont, with one last message for Queen Bee

Madison's knees buckled, and Felicity reached for her hand and squeezed it tight.

Jack cleared his throat. "Thanks for giving me a few minutes this morning to come on here and read my latest letter to Queen Bee. I hope you don't mind, but I've written it in the form of a list."

A listicle?

A hysterical burst of laughter escaped Madison's lips. Was she dreaming? How could this be real?

Jack glanced down at a piece of paper in his hands.

"So without further ado, here are the top ten reasons Fired Up in Lovestruck is in love with Queen Bee."

"Oh, my God. I remember hearing about this." An editorial assistant from the fashion department gestured to Madison with her coffee cup. "You're Queen Bee, aren ι you? He's talking to *you*."

"Shhh! We need to hear." Felicity gave Madison's hand another squeeze, which was a good thing because her support was the sole reason Madison was still upright.

Jack was in love with her and he'd managed to get himself onto national television just to win her back.

That was what was happening, wasn't it?

She tried to tamp down the happiness sparkling inside her, just in case…just in case she was dreaming or had somehow misunderstood things. Just in case this was all part of some really elaborate good-bye instead of what she so desperately hoped it was. A new beginning.

She thought she might faint, but she couldn't— not without hearing his list. He hadn't even started reading it yet, and she could already feel her face splitting into a goofy smile.

"Number one: she loves with her whole heart, even when she's trying not to."

Madison's breath hitched. He'd cut straight to her soul right off the bat.

"Number two: she has excellent taste in bedtime

stories. Number three: the sound of her voice when I can't sleep at night." He looked right into the camera again, and the sheer vulnerability in his gaze left no mistake—this wasn't just an elaborate goodbye. He was opening up to her in a way he never had before.

She inhaled a ragged breath, tears clouding her vision as he went on.

"Number four: she's the best knitter I know." A secret smile tipped his lips, and Madison laughed. "Number five: children and animals love her, even when she's afraid they won't. Number six: I love the way her pink toenails perfectly match the polka dots on her bathrobe. Number seven: I love her untamed hair."

Felicity and the editorial assistants cast confused glances at Madison's carefully flat-ironed do, as did about half a dozen other *Fashionista* staffers who'd wandered into the break room since Jack began reciting his list.

Madison barely noticed their curious stares. She was rooted to the spot, hanging on Jack's every word, pressing her hand to her heart as if she could tuck everything he said deep inside where she could take his words out and replay them again later. Over and over.

On the screen he took a deep breath, and the sheet of paper in his hands trembled ever so slightly. "Number eight: she's the bravest, most beautiful person I've ever met. Number nine: my girls miss her. *I* miss her."

Madison sank down into the closest chair. She could barely see Jack's face on the screen anymore, because she'd begun crying in earnest.

"I knew it," Felicity said quietly beside her. "He misses you, too."

"And number ten?" Meghan prompted onscreen as she dabbed at the corners of her eyes with a tissue. "What's the last one, Fired Up?"

"Number ten is the simplest one. I love her for the same reason I love Vermont—she always smells like apples and fresh air." He looked up from the list, and his eyes shone brighter than Madison had ever seen them before. Forget-me-not blue. "Like home."

Everything that happened next seemed to pass in a blur—Meghan gushing over Jack's letter, the camera switching to a cooking segment before Madison could fully register what she'd just witnessed, the oohs and ahhs of her coworkers, especially Felicity who'd darted back to their cubicle and returned with Madison's handbag and a pair of ballerina flats from the fashion closet.

"Here. You're going to need these." She thrust the items toward Madison. "If you hurry, you can make it to the studio before Jack leaves. You *are* going after him, aren't you?"

Felicity's sense of urgency pulled Madison out of her dreamy little trance. He was right there in New York. In the midst of all the shock and excitement of what he'd just done, that significant detail hadn't even registered in her consciousness.

Madison nodded. Every cell in her body screamed. *Yes! Yes, yes, yes.* Of course she was going after him.

She kicked off her Jimmy Choo shoes and slid into the ballet flats. They were pink, just like the polka dots on the bathrobe that she couldn't believe Jack remembered when he'd only seen her in it once.

As she stood and slung her purse over her shoulder, the happy chatter in the break room came to an abrupt end, replaced by an awkward silence. All eyes turned toward the doorway, where Angelica Kent, resplendent in a floral Erdem dress Madison had last seen on Kate Middleton, stood with her arms crossed and a scowl on her face.

"Well, well, I wondered where our entire staff had gone," she said. "Everyone, get back to work."

Felicity and the others scattered in a flurry of clicking heels and a swish of fine fabric, leaving Madison alone in her handmade sweater and flat shoes to deal with Angelica.

Her boss eyed her from head to toe, and Madison had never missed Mr. Grant and his brown tie so much in her life. "That means you, too, Madison."

"I'm sorry, Angelica. Thank you for the opportunity." Joy like she'd never known filled Madison's chest. She was going back to Lovestruck—back to Jack and his girls. Back to Alice and Toby and the town where she'd left her heart. Vermont didn't hate her. It never had, but it had changed her and that was where she belonged. Now and forever. "But I quit."

One minute, Jack was sitting on the big orange sofa on the *Good Morning Sunshine* set with a camera in his face, and the next...

Nothing.

He was pretty sure that Meghan Ashley and the producer, who apparently had family in Lovestruck, both shook his hand and thanked him for appearing on the show, but everything happened so fast, he couldn't remember a word either of them had said. The cameras vanished, moving to the opposite side of the room in a flash, where a cookbook author was busy whipping up a gluten-free alternative to traditional tacos. A production assistant unclipped the microphone from his lapel, talking a mile a minute as she did so. When Jack tried to respond to a question she'd just asked, she shook her head and tapped the sleek black earpiece attached to her head. She hadn't even been speaking to him.

No one was. The great mystery of Fired Up in Lovestruck had been solved, and apparently, everyone had moved on to something else with lightning speed. Jack had been longing for this exact scenario for *weeks*, but now that it was finally happening, he felt empty all of a sudden.

Empty…and more alone than he'd ever been in his entire life.

But what could he have possibly expected? It wasn't as if Madison would see him on television, drop everything she was doing and come find him. That was so far beyond what he'd allowed himself to hope that it was laughable. He just hoped she'd somehow see the segment, or maybe read about it in the *Bee*. Perhaps her aunt Alice would send her a copy of the front-page article Floyd Grant was planning to run, wrapping up the whole saga of Queen Bee and Fired Up in Lovestruck with a nice, tidy bow. Jack had answered each and every question the editor-in-chief had asked him. He'd pledged his full cooperation in exchange for the most public platform possible to tell Madison how he really felt about her, and Floyd Grant had gotten him to New York and on television within three hours.

And now here he was, trying to navigate his way out of the maze of a national broadcasting company all on his own so he could get back to Lovestruck and his twins in time for his mom to get to her knitting class at Main Street Yarn.

A security guard took mercy on him, escorted him to the elevator and left him with directions on how to get to the exit. Once he reached the ground floor, he removed the name badge and security clearance from around his neck, returned them to the guard station and pushed his way through the smoked glass double doors.

The sun glinting off the surrounding skyscrapers was almost blinding. Jack stood for a second, disoriented by the city's assault on his senses. Manhattan was everything that Lovestruck wasn't—bustling, expansive, exhilarating. It thrummed like a great big beating heart, and he could see why Madison loved it so much. He knew better than to hope she'd come back to Vermont, and that was okay. Really, it was. He just wanted a chance to love her the way she deserved to be loved. They could make it work, somehow. He didn't have a plan, but he was willing to move heaven and earth to figure it out.

If it was what Madison wanted.

If it wasn't?

Jack's chest ached as if there was nothing but a hole where his heart had once been. He didn't want to consider that possibility—not until he was back in Lovestruck where he could lick his wounds and try and figure out a way to get on with his life.

He turned in the direction of the cabstand on the corner, but just as he took his first step, he thought he heard his name above the din of the honking horns, siren wails and street noises that were all part of the unique music of Manhattan. He paused, certain his mind was playing on tricks on him, because that lovely lilt had sounded an awful lot like…

"Madison?" He squinted into the sunlight.

And all of a sudden, there she was, walking toward him like something out of a dream—an angel with wind-tossed hair and eyes as warm as autumn in Vermont. Voice like a lullaby.

Her footsteps slowed to a stop about ten feet away from him. She looked smaller than he'd remembered, daintier somehow. And then he realized she was wearing flat shoes instead of the towering heels she'd always worn to wobble her way around Lovestruck. He studied them for a second, cocking his head, and when he looked back up, their gazes locked.

Jack reached into the side pocket of his cargo pants and pulled out the apple he'd brought with him—the one from the fire station. He offered it to her as if it was a Valentine. As if it was his heart.

Madison launched herself at him then, crashing into his arms with such force that he nearly toppled over. So he held on to her as tightly as he could, whispering each and every item from his list into her hair, not for an audience this time, but just for them. Just for her.

And when he was finished, right before she pressed her lips to his, she smiled and whispered the words that were the best sort of balm to his aching heart. "Take me home, hero. Take me home to Lovestruck."

The Lovestruck Bee

Wedding Announcements

Jules/Cole

On Saturday, December 25, Madison Jules, familiar to readers of this newspaper as our parenting columnist and newly appointed fashion editor Queen Bee, married Lieutenant Jack Cole of the Lovestruck Fire Department. Lieutenant Cole is known nationwide as Fired Up in Lovestruck, devoted dad, letter-writing enthusiast and Queen Bee's number-one fan.

The wedding took place at Lovestruck Community Church on Main Street, and was attended by Jason "Cap" Anderson, who together with Alice Jules, gave the bride away. The groom's eight-month-old twin daughters served as honorary flower girls, while Toby the Chinese crested acted as ring bearer. The bride has asked us to be sure and note that Emma and Ella Cole were dressed in delicate white tulle by Vera Wang, a recent fan of Queen Bee and Fired Up in Lovestruck's letters to the editor, and that Toby the dog "stunned in a hand-knitted dog tuxedo of angora yarn and a collar made from fresh flowers."

Wade Ericson of the LFD stood as best man, alongside maid of honor, Felicity Hart of New York City. The reception was held at the Mansion on Orchard Drive, where guests dined on vanilla apple wedding cake with but-tercream frosting and red-apple martinis.

The couple is registered at Sephora.
The Lovestruck Bee

The editor-in-chief has been asked to print the following correction to yesterday's Jules/ Cole wedding announcement:
Maid of Honor Felicity Hart is no longer a resident of New York City and now has plans to relocate to Lovestruck because "it's as cute as a button and she's always had a thing for firemen."

* * * * *

Don't miss Teri Wilson's next book in the Lovestruck, Vermont miniseries, available December 2020 from Harlequin Special Edition!